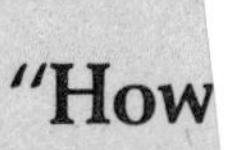

Ryan sp... bathroom doorway. He wore only a towel...and a delicious smile. "I'd find out for myself, but you did say an 'uninterrupted' soak."

"A woman's entitled to change her mind...." Already Cecily could feel the warm honey stealing through her. When he dropped his towel, her roving eyes took in the strength of his need for her.

Then her breasts were being pressed against his chest, and he was licking droplets from her skin. "Water's fine," he murmured against her ear. "Now to make sure I approve of its effect on you..."

Cecily giggled as his fingers tickled her back, her ribs. The giggle became a sigh when Ryan deepened his open-mouthed kisses, when his tongue nudged her wet nipples. His hand roamed to her thighs, and greedily she pulled him under....

THE AUTHOR

When Evelyn Shannon told her computer repairman what her book was about, he just shook his head and said, "You don't look like no motorcycle mama to me." But even if she doesn't, Evelyn is happy to introduce unusual ideas into her romances. She is unusual altogether, having memorized *Julius Caesar* by age five.

Under the names Sharon Frances and Francine Shore, she has published other contemporary romances, as well as historicals under the Cynthia Sinclair pseudonym. Evelyn lives with her husband and two grown sons in Massachusetts.

Two for the Road

EVELYN SHANNON

Harlequin Books

TORONTO • NEW YORK • LONDON
AMSTERDAM • PARIS • SYDNEY • HAMBURG
STOCKHOLM • ATHENS • TOKYO • MILAN

Published November 1985

ISBN 0-373-25184-X

Printed in Canada

1

"COME ON, Zolichick!"

Eyes narrowed against the dust and exhaust, Cecily stood on tiptoe and craned her neck for a better view as the two lead motorcyclists zoomed by. Both of them were riding tucked in, with arms and legs squeezed into the frames of their cycles, but Matt Zolichick's BMW was inches in front of the Motor Guzzi.

"Come on, hotshoe!" she cried. "Go for it!"

"He's going to open some space right now," a deep voice commented behind her.

She nodded eagerly. "He sure is—there. He's got the lead now. If he just holds it, he'll win this event."

"The man on the Italian bike is falling behind." Cecily craned her neck still farther, but couldn't see past the broad shoulders of the large man who had stepped in front of her. As she maneuvered for some kind of view, she found herself caught at the waist and lifted up. "That better?"

She didn't have time for more than a breathless thanks, for her eyes were on the race. As the BMW swept across the finish line well ahead of the Motor Guzzi, she sighed in heartfelt appreciation.

"Your friend ran a Grand Prix race," the man with the deep voice agreed.

"Thanks for the boost...." Cecily turned her head as she spoke, and looked back into interested, dark-lashed gray eyes. He was tall—had to be, for at nearly a foot off the ground she was eye-to-eye with him—and those eyes reminded her of the clear, sun-bright gray of the sea. But perhaps it was a trick of the light that found blue highlights in the waving dark hair and softened the strong, hard-planed face. She had the confused thought that perhaps the breathlessness sweeping through her resulted from his still holding her suspended. It couldn't stem from the fact that this was the most unsconscionably handsome man she'd ever seen.

He lowered her to the ground but kept his hands at her waist. Pressed close against him amid the throng who'd come to watch the Sunday Jedborough Motorcycle Road Race, her sense of imbalance grew. It was almost as if she'd stepped into weightless, airless space. To counter the feeling, she faced him and spoke briskly. "This was Matt Zolichick's first real road race. My father taught him to ride as a little kid, and even though Matt's now a U of Mass student—majoring in economics yet—racing is his number-one love. This race had him so nervous that I promised his girlfriend and him I'd come to Jedborough to give moral support."

"He had a shaky first lap, but he recovered in the second, and his third and fourth were scorching. But, then, anyone taught by Art Leeds has to be a winner."

"You know Art, then?" Surprised, Cecily realized there was something familiar about the man's fine-featured face, the tall and powerful form blessed with the natural poise of an athlete. She'd seen him somewhere—but where? "Are you a racer?" she asked.

"No, but Art Leeds has been a hero of mine since I was a youngster. My name is Ryan Alexander. I watched your father race in Daytona when he won the short track, and again at Santa Fe. I also made it to Japan a few years ago, when his bike had that problem with the gearbox and he just missed winning the Japanese Grand Prix."

Her green eyes went wide with pleasure. "You were actually there? I envy you! I was in school, and Art wouldn't take me out to go with him overseas. How did he race? I've seen the tapes, of course, but they're not the real thing."

"He was great. It was as if he and that cycle were fused." The sea-gray eyes silvered with enthusiasm, but before he could say more there was a whoop behind them, and Cecily turned to see Matt Zolichick and his Peggy, hurrying toward her.

She met them halfway, and was nearly crushed in Matt's bear hug. "It wasn't me that won—it was Art's teaching and your cheering me on that did it." Matt was nearly beside himself with excitement. He accepted Ryan Alexander's congratulations, then turned back to Cecily to say, "I'll take the 'battle of the twins' event easily. Peggy clocked my lap times as better than I've ever run before."

"We'd better check your machine," Cecily pointed out, and Matt came out of the clouds long enough to admit that the clutch could be slipping a little, before he returned to a blow-by-blow description of the race. Peggy gazed at him adoringly. As Cecily went to the pit area and knelt to remove the clutch cover, she found that Ryan Alexander had hunkered down beside her. The movement called attention to the solid thigh muscles that strained the well-fitting designer jeans.

"Need any help?" he asked.

"Only if you want to hand me the rag over there—and that screwdriver." As he obliged, she realized how attentively Ryan was watching her. She tried to concentrate on what she was doing, adjusting the clutch before turning her attention to the clutch cable on the handlebars, while Matt checked his tire pressure and shocks. But it was hard to work efficiently under that clear gray gaze. Perhaps, she thought, he was an ace mechanic, which was why he looked so tantalizingly familiar. She ventured a quick look up at him and then veiled her eyes with her long, thick lashes when she saw that he'd caught her in the act. He was smiling. In sudden confusion, she lifted an uncertain hand to push back a strand of red-gold hair that had escaped the confines of her businesslike chignon. "Tantalizing" was the word for him.

"You did that very professionally," he said when Matt had taken his BMW and gone with Peggy to await their next event. "But, then, I should have expected Art Leeds's daughter to be what's called a 'good wrench.' I worked up a thirst just watching you. Would you go for a cold beer?"

She couldn't help a chuckle. "This isn't Daytona, Ryan." She nodded to a creaky stand nearby, which had been mobbed by the crowd seeking soft drinks, coffee, hot dogs and hamburgers. "That's as close as you'll get to a cold beer, I'm afraid."

His grin was infectious. "Come with me, and you'll see."

Had the man come equipped for a tailgate picnic? Curious, Cecily followed him from the spectator's area to the adjacent parking lot. When she saw where he was leading her, she gulped. "Oh," she said. "Wow..."

The Harley-Davidson FLTC Electra Glide Classic was parked near the entrance to the parking lot, arrogantly aloof from the other cycles and the vans and cars, its windjammer thrust forward in proud power. She ran her hand lightly over the coal-black body. It seemed to sense her admiration and purred like a panther.

"It's one beautiful hunk of machine." She knelt to look at the powerful wheels, then up at Ryan. "You had it custom-built, didn't you?"

"I needed certain specifications met."

Who was he that he could afford to spend that kind of money?

"Want to see how the engine responds?" he went on. "There's a tavern down the street with ice-cold beer."

She hesitated, but the contest was unequal. Art would never forgive her if she didn't try out this luxurious customized machine. Matt's next event was some time away, and a cold beer would hit the spot.

"Good." Ryan Alexander acted as if he'd followed her rationalizing and was amused by it. "I'll bring you back in time to cheer Matt on. Trust me."

Cecily had left her helmet in the pit area with her own motorcycle, a lovingly cared for '68 Harley-Davidson Sportster. When she returned, he was already mounted on his Electra Glide. Astride it, he looked as arrogant as the cycle itself, helmeted head lifted proudly, shoulders a powerful wedge against the light. She found herself catching an involuntary breath, and then was surprised at her own reaction. After all, she had test ridden countless motorcycles before. As she took her place behind him and adjusted her helmet, she told herself this was just another such test drive.

Dark goggles shuttered his eyes when he turned to her. "I want you to see how powerful this machine is, so I'm going to accelerate fast, all right?"

She wrapped her arms around his waist. "Go."

His acceleration was skillful—both smooth and strong. She felt the rush of wind velocity and tried to listen to and feel the full power of the V2-Evolution engine, but her attention wouldn't stay with the Electra Glide. She was sidetracked by acute awareness of the whipcord-lean, sinewy body she was pressed against.

They went wide into a corner, and she thought less of the machine's responsivenss than of her own body's reaction to the play of back muscles hugged tightly to her high breasts. And against the sensitive palms of her hand she felt the ripple of silk and steel—the muscles of his lean waist and taut belly. The blue and gold and green of the September day whooshed past her, and mingling with the scent of dust was the clean, virile scent of this man close to her. She shut her eyes, feeling herself totally enveloped in speed and power and the fragrance of Ryan Alexander. It was almost as if they had left the earth and were soaring aloft.

"We're here." His matter-of-fact voice, coupled with the slowing of the cycle, broke the spell. She opened her eyes. They had reached the small tavern in the bend of the road.

"That was some ride." She was still feeling shaky as he braked smoothly, and she warned herself to ease up. It must have been the exhilarating speed of the Electra Glide that had so moved her. "Art would have enjoyed it—and been able to tell you a lot more about it than I can. It's a powerful machine, and it handles wonderfully well."

"Thanks for those kind words, ma'am. Where is your father, anyway? If Matt is a protégé of his, wouldn't he want to see him race?"

"He's in New Hampshire. He was going to come to Jedborough today, but at the last moment one of our customers commissioned him to go along to the Frank Wells Road Race as his mechanic. It's an important local competition, just steps below the big one in Laconia."

"I suppose you get many contracts like that." He held the tavern door open for her. "I heard that when your father retired from racing, he started Leeds Motorcycles in Clinton. That's about an hour southwest of Boston, isn't it?"

"Yes." As she passed him she was again aware of his powerful masculinity. Without touching him, she could sense the hardness of his chest overlaid with crisp curly hair that just showed at the opening of his white shirt. Disturbed by where her thoughts were taking her, she glanced up at him and saw that he was watching her once more. The warm and interested glint in the silver-gray eyes made her feel slightly giddy.

Cicily was grateful when they were seated and separate, even if only by the length of the small tavern table. "Actually," she told him, "we started Leeds Motorcycles long before Art gave up racing. He was always an expert motorcycle mechanic, and he taught me the craft. We both loved cycles so much it seemed natural that we'd want to get into a business connected with them somehow." He nodded agreement, and she added, "It's really a small garage built in the backyard of our home in Clinton. We had dreams of expanding it, starting a motorcycle-riding school."

"But?" he prompted as she hesitated.

"Art can be impractical," she said slowly. "Artists are, I guess. He loves old motorcycles, and he buys and rebuilds them with the hope of selling them—then lets them go for a song. Or he'll feel sorry for a customer and tear up a bill. He drives George wild."

Ryan smiled. "Should I ask who George is?"

"He's Matt's father and our accountant. The nicest man who ever lived and the biggest pessimist."

The beer arrived, cool and golden and white foamed. The first gulp was frosty and delicious, making Cecily wonder why even her appreciation of a simple glass of beer seemed heightened today.

"I wouldn't think there's a man alive who could be down with you around." He said that almost casually, but she intuited that he meant it.

"George thinks we could do more business." Then realizing she shouldn't be sitting here talking shop to this obviously wealthy stranger, she tried another tack. "George is family, actually. He and his wife took charge of me when Art had to go on the racing circuit after my mother died."

"Losing your mother must have been hard on you."

The unexpected gentleness in his voice surprised her. She hadn't meant to do so, but she found herself saying, "We were very close. You hear about mothers and daughters not getting on, but we really loved each other. People even said we looked like each other. When she...was taken in an automobile accident, Art was in England participating in the races on the Isle of Man. I managed to hang together somehow until he got home only because of George and Edna Zolichick."

She couldn't go on. And in the silence that followed, it seemed almost as if she didn't have to, that Ryan knew without being told of the loneliness that had clung to her heart like ashes, of the memories that had prevented the wounds from healing. How could he know this, when he knew little else about her, she wondered. All thought fell away as he reached across the small pine-grained table between them and rubbed his thumb lightly across her knuckles.

The gesture was as friendly and as warm as a handclasp, and Cecily realized she was relaxing under his touch. "But even if there was so much grief, you remembered the good times. That helped, didn't it?"

The tone of his voice surprised her, because it was almost wistful. Looking up, she saw for a moment a shadow pass across his strong features. "Good times always help," she agreed. "Besides, Art and I were very close, even when I went to U of Mass to study mechanical engineering. Weekends, breaks—whenever I could I always seemed to make it home."

He nodded understanding. "Did you ever want to race, too?"

She watched the white foam settling on her beer. "Not really. I've always loved motorcycles, of course, and I could take one apart a long time before I was old enough to actually ride one." She smiled as she added, "Motorcycle touring has always been my dream, though. You know, the grand and glamorous tours you see advertised for cyclists in England and Tokyo and Spain. Art and I used to sit on the couch in the living room with an atlas between us and dream of traveling together to the far corners of the earth."

"And did you?"

She chuckled ruefully, shook her head. "We're still dreaming."

"Could be you've been waiting for the right tour to come along." He reached back into the pocket of his designer jeans and drew out a slim, expensive-looking wallet, flipped it open and extracted a card. "Perhaps you've heard of Ryan A. Tours?"

His tanned fingers brushed hers as she took the card from him, but the jolt she felt had nothing to do with that touch. " 'Ryan A. Tours'—Ryan Alexander," she muttered, as her dammed-up memory suddenly released the information. "Of course I've seen you before. Your father is Desmond Alexander of Alexander Industries...."

"Ryan A. Tours has nothing to do with Alexander Industries."

So engrossed was she in remembering that she didn't register the slight tightening of his fine mouth. "You were interviewed on 'Sixty Seconds,' weren't you? And *Sport* magazine did a cover on your latest tour—an expedition over the Alps. You and your tour members set out to recreate Hannibal's crossing."

"You have a good memory."

"Only because your tour sounded so different from anything I'd ever heard of."

He leaned back in his chair. "I hope your father feels that way. I've been looking for him—came to Jedborough because I was told he'd be here, in fact. I wanted to see if he'd be interested in a business proposition. My company is offering a three-week motorcycle adventure in the spring. We'll cross the New Hampshire White Mountains, follow an historic and scenic route into Vermont and New York, and finish with an exploration of the Pine Barrens of New Jersey."

"It sounds exciting, but how would that involve Art?" she asked.

"In order to pave the way for the tour, I'm going on a trailblazing expedition soon. I'm no mechanic, so I need to hire an expert on motorcycles to go along with me. Art is not only an expert, but his name still carries a lot of magic from his racing days." He paused as if to emphasize the point, then added, "I want that magic associated with my spring tour."

She knew how much such a trip would mean to Art. She could visualize his joy as he watched the sun shining on the Kankamagus Highway, the foliage changing as they traveled through Vermont, then the mysterious forests of the New Jersey Barrens. And the money...money enough to keep even George quiet and happy.

Ryan was smiling as if Art's acceptance were a foregone conclusion, which for some reason bothered Cecily. There was such a contrast between Leeds Motorcycles and the vigor and wealth of Ryan A. Tours, personified by Ryan's own strength. She restrained a sigh as she shook her head.

"He can't do it." That wasn't the answer Ryan Alexander had expected to hear, obviously. Dark eyebrows rose quizzically, and regret and unhappiness made her voice stiff. "He hasn't been well. All those falls while he was racing—they bother him now, and in the mornings he has terrible arthritis. This morning he could hardly hold the steering wheel of his van. There's no way he could physically handle such a long trip."

"Perhaps I'd better speak to him myself," Ryan said.

Did he think she was acting like an overprotective mother hen? She hesitated before saying, "I wish you wouldn't. Hearing of the tour would just make him unhappy, because he really couldn't make it physically. And now we'd better hotfoot it back to the track if we're to watch Matt race."

He seemed thoughtful as they left the tavern, and so was she. Exhilaration had faded in the face of grim reality. In spite of what she'd said, she was sure Ryan would approach Art about the tour. He'd come to Clinton and make Art feel wretched and old. After all, supremely wealthy men played by their own rules, never expecting anyone to gainsay them in anything. Though she wasn't familiar with the financial world, she knew the Alexanders were worth several fortunes with interests in engineering, oil and computers. No wonder Ryan could come to a small-time motorcycle road race on a custom-built Electra Glide that had to have cost a small fortune itself.

Cecily tried to shake off such thoughts. Yet when they returned to the track, where riders of two-cylinder motorcycles were taking their positions to compete in the "battle of the twins," she saw things as Ryan Alexander must see them. The track surrounded by a narrow concrete wall was lackluster and third-rate, and even Matt's precious and carefully maintained BMW looked shabby. She winced a little as Ryan nodded to a cycle beside Matt's. "What kind of bike is that supposed to be?"

"Café Rider," she said; the wry lift of his eyebrows further depressed her. What could a man like Ryan know of making do? How could he sympathize with the painstaking use of clip-ons to make an ordinary street bike look like an expensive racer? "Sometimes Café Riders can be pretty good competition." She heard the defensiveness in her voice.

Neither pursued that subject as they went to stand near the pit area. Peggy came over to stand beside them. "Matt's really psyched for this one," she announced. "He said to tell you he was going to leave them all standing."

The signal was given, and the contestants roared down the track. As they made the quarter turn, Matt was definitely in the lead. The man on the Café Rider followed him closely.

"He's going to try a zap!" Cecily heard an onlooker shout.

Tucked in tightly, the Café Rider attempted to pass Matt as they came around the bend of the first lap. Peggy shouted excitedly, but Cecily frowned. Matt's timing was off. "Something's wrong," she muttered.

"Good God, he's going into a skid!"

As Ryan spoke, Peggy screamed. Cecily watched in silent horror as Matt tried desperately to control his cycle. He barely missed hitting the Café Rider beside him, and then headed straight for the narrow wall that ran alongside the track. Next moment, the cycle had collided with concrete—Matt had flipped end over end and landed on the ground.

The other motorcyclists zoomed past as Cecily started to run toward Matt. Ryan was quicker. From the corner of her eye, Cecily saw him move in a purposeful blur, vaulting the wall and racing downtrack to where Matt lay. Ryan was already leaning over the prone rider by the time she reached them. "He's all right," Ryan assured her. "He's gotten the wind knocked out of him, and he may have a broken rib or two but he hasn't damaged anything that won't mend."

"Thank God." Art had told her of races in which cyclists were killed, and she'd seen terrible injuries herself. Matt, however, wasn't in any mood for thanksgiving. As Cecily knelt in the dust by his side, she saw that he was close to tears.

"I endoed," he groaned bitterly. "I actually did a stupid endo. Cecily, is my bike busted?"

He struggled to get up; Ryan pushed him gently down again. "Easy, pal. Cecily will check out your cycle for you. Meanwhile, we've got to get you some help."

In the near distance they could hear the wail of an ambulance, and paramedics came hurrying up. Matt was placed on a stretcher. Ryan accompanied an almost-hysterical Peggy to the ambulance, but knowing how much Matt's BMW meant to him, Cecily remained behind to push the bike to the safety of the pit. She was checking it over, when Ryan came back to report that Peggy had accompanied Matt to the Jedborough hospital. "They want to take some X rays. Matt didn't want to go. He kept saying he wanted to stick around and hear what happened to his cycle."

"It's got a bent fork, and the frame will need work. That skid wasn't his fault, by the way. He had a plug wire break on him." Cecily frowned at the wire as she remembered all the young man's hopes. "Poor Matt."

"There'll be other races." He spoke so casually that her irritation increased.

"I suppose that to you one ruined motorcycle isn't a tragedy. Matt's a college student, a struggling young racer. He can't afford crack-ups like this."

"Are you saying Leeds Motorcycles can't save this BMW?" There was an odd glitter in his eyes and a challenge in his deep voice. "You're throwing in the towel?"

She raised her softly rounded chin and spoke firmly. "Don't make book on it, mister. Art and I will make this poor old cycle sing again, and he'll win again, too. He really is a hotshoe—a talented racer. One of these days you'll be in your millionaire's box at a Grand Prix—and see him take the prize."

There was silence for the space of a heartbeat. Then Ryan whistled softly. "By George, she's got what it takes. You'll do, Cecily."

She threw back her head and stared up at him, raising her dusty hand to shade her eyes. He looked pleased with himself and—smug. Decidedly smug.

"What are you talking about?" she demanded.

"It's too bad about your father, but maybe this will work out even better. You're Art's daughter, after all." He reached down, took both her hands and drew her to her feet.

She tugged herself loose glaring at him. "I don't understand a word you're saying."

His satisfaction and his smile deepended. "I'm talking about the tour, of course. Obviously I'm hiring you to go with me all the way to the Pine Barrens and beyond. Get packed, Cecily. We leave in a week."

2

FOR A MOMENT she was too taken aback to do more than stare at him, speechless. He continued to smile down at her, pleased as hell. "I'll have to make some changes, but nothing major. There'll be women cyclists in the tour party, so your feedback would be helpful to me. You might have some suggestions already."

"Only one," she said. "You'd better get someone else."

To her annoyance, he laughed, "Really," he said.

"I mean it. I couldn't be right for the job."

"Don't put yourself down that way," he told her kindly. "I realize you haven't had much touring experience, but that doesn't matter. I can see you're a good mechanic, and that's what counts. Besides, you've dreamed of something like this—you told me so, back at the tavern. Think of riding into a sunrise over the Kittatiny Mountains. Think of the cool mysterious depths of the Pine Barrens...."

It wasn't fair, she thought, that he was using what she'd told him of her and Art's dreams to get his way. "I'm really not interested."

Dark eyebrows quirked upward. "Afraid of what the neighbors would say?"

Holding her rising indignation in check, she explained, "I couldn't leave Art alone for three weeks—as I told you, he's not well these days."

"Nonsense. You could hire temporary help. Matt Zolichick would be able to lend a hand by then, and even if he couldn't, I'd bet there are twenty aspiring cyclists eager to work for next to nothing just so they could learn from Art Leeds." Ryan reached out, almost, but not quite, running his hand up her bare arm in a shadow touch that brushed static electricity over her skin.

Abruptly she pulled away and began pushing Matt's motorcycle toward the parking lot. "Even if that were true, you're overlooking something terribly important. Motorcycles have been Art's life. It hurt him terribly when he had to retire from racing, and it will break his heart to realize he can't even go on tour anymore. My accepting your offer would be like rubbing salt in the wound."

He walked silently beside her for a few moments before he said, "I can understand how Art might feel, but shouldn't you at least ask how much I'm prepared to pay? Perhaps to Leeds Motorcycles three hundred dollars a day sounds like chicken feed, but I'd also throw in a bonus at the end of the trip and offer a three-thousand-dollar kill fee if the project scrubs out before the halfway mark."

Over six thousand dollars for three weeks' work! Cecily stopped pushing Matt's cycle. Ryan smiled down at her. "Lighten up, Cecily. What really worries you about riding off into the wilderness with me for three weeks? You know we'd be too busy mapping routes and riding for any other, ah, more pleasurable activities. Besides, I've never forced myself on any unwilling female."

"The possibility never even entered my mind," she snapped. "And now, if you'll excuse me—I do have a few things to do before getting up to the hospital to see how Matt's doing."

"Think about it," Ryan advised her. "Discuss it with your father. As I said, I want the Leeds name associated with this tour. I'll be in my Boston office for the next few days, getting ready for the trip, so you can call me there with your decision."

He sounded sure of her capitulation. And why shouldn't he feel sure of himself? He was rich and successful, and he probably felt he was doing her a big favor by offering to allow her to take her father's place. He probably felt that everyone had a price. She wanted to take him by those broad shoulders and shake him. Instead she turned to face him and spoke very deliberately. "All right, I'll think about it. But I won't change my mind, Mr. Alexander. Don't hold your breath waiting."

His gray eyes were full of silver sunlight as he reached out and tucked a strand of errant red-gold hair behind Cecily's ear. She jerked her head away, but undaunted, he very lightly traced his fingers over the contour of her jaw and chin. Wanting to ignore him, she found she couldn't. What was more, he knew it, for his smile was warm, confident, totally provocative.

"Some things," he told her, "are worth waiting for."

"GEORGE, ARE YOU SURE it's okay for Matt to be out of the hospital?" Art Leeds wanted to know as he ran gnarled, knowledgeable hands over the bent fork of Matt Zolichick's BMW. "Ceci says he took a good endo Sunday. Here it's only Tuesday, and he's already home and running around."

George nodded. "The X rays didn't even show any breaks—he's just got a few bone bruises. Youth is wonderful."

"Last time I endoed was in Laconia...or was it at Sante Fe? I fractured my pelvis on that little trip through the air." Art Leeds rubbed his hip with a reminiscent wince. "George, you were lucky Ceci was there."

"The paramedics took over—" she began, but Art shook his graying head.

"The paramedics took care of Matt's body. You took charge of his cycle, and to a biker that's the most important thing." He paused and then said unexpectedly, "You know, Ceci, it's a rare woman who knows what's most important to a man. Your mother had that gift, too, God rest her."

Late-afternoon sunlight was pouring through the open doors into Leeds Motorcycles' small shop, and when she looked away from Art her eyes were dazzled with it. Coupled with the ache that came at the mention of her mother was a twinge of guilt. Art was right about one thing: Cecily knew what was important in his life. She glanced over the rows of motorcycles brought in for repair, the many used cycles Art kept buying to rebuild for resale and the usual assortment of tools and spare parts. The familiar smells of oil and cleanser and metal and leather permeated everything. Over where the two men stood, in the small corner that was used for an office, hung the dusty framed photographs of Art Leeds in his moments of greatest triumph.

"I didn't come out here to talk about Matt. You've got problems," George was saying. He tugged at his small mustache. He was a florid-faced little man, as portly as Art was slim, and his mustache was his weather vein. When it was sleek and smooth, all was well; when it bristled, or when he pulled it, trouble was in the air.

Art made a face. "George, you're an old lady in pants. If you went outside and there was a drop of rain, you'd swear the sky was falling."

George growled, and Cecily's heart sank. "How badly in the hole are we now?" she asked.

"As your accountant, I'd say you were up the creek without a paddle. You owe money you don't have, and your cash flow is almost nonexistent. Besides which, quarterlies are due on your taxes—how you're going to pay them, God knows."

"But that's not possible." Cecily frowned as she turned to her father. "We were going to settle up our debts and be in the clear when we were paid for the last big job we did...." Art's eyes didn't meet her's. "Wasn't that what we planned?"

A vicious tweak made George's mustache look like a bird's nest. "You know Art, Cecily. He's always falling for sob stories from bikers who say they can't pay. This last one bilked Leeds Motorcycles out of hundreds of dollars, the dollars that were going to help you get squared away."

"It wasn't that bad." Because her father still couldn't look her in the eye, Cecily knew the situation was worse. "If I can't give a hand to someone down on his luck..."

George turned bright red and shouted. "How about helping yourself for a change? Or your daughter? She's not an old fossil like you—she's only twenty-five, and she has good looks and brains, and she should have the world on her plate. Why should she have to work all the time in this rinky-dink shop, for God's sakes, when you could be running a sensible business and showing a profit?" Art opened his mouth to answer, but George wasn't finished. "As if that isn't bad enough, you have to be an impulse buyer. Look at that hunk of tin you went and bought yesterday on the way home from the races."

"It's an old Ducati 750SS Clubman Racer, you ignoramus," Art sputtered, getting excited in turn. "Sure it's a mess now, but do you know what it will be worth when I get it fixed up?" He turned to Cecily. "I didn't have a chance to tell you, but she's a beauty, and I got her for a song—"

"Try a prayer," George snarled. "You'll need it."

Cecily interposed hastily, "Perhaps we could get a bank loan."

"And maybe they sell snowballs in hell," George grumbled. "The trouble is, Cecily, your credit is all shot. Your house is remortgaged. The shop is remortgaged. You don't have any assets worth a damn." He swung wrathfully on Art. "And don't you tell me that Ducati-whatever-it-is is an asset, either, because I know it'll cost more to fix than it will get when it sells." He shook his finger in Art's face. "You don't have any options left. And yet you give handouts and buy old motorcycles on credit. You'll end up losing everything you worked for, don't you see that?"

There was a horrible pause. Into it came a discreet cough and a pleasant tenor voice asking, "Excuse me, but is this Leeds Motorcycles?"

Cecily swung around with the others, and was both grateful and embarrassed to see a stranger standing in the doorway of the shop. He wore a three-piece suit, and the hand he extended to her had recently be manicured.

"Mr. Art Leeds?" Pale-blue eyes behind wire-rimmed glasses hovered over Cecily, passed George's still-crimson face and settled on Art. "I'm Leonard Coxe from *Intro* magazine. Perhaps you've heard of us?"

Who hadn't? Into Cecily's mind flashed the slogan of the Boston-based national magazine read by millions across the country and around the world: if you haven't read *Intro*, you're only half informed.... September's issue had featured interviews with top financiers; last month's had offered a thoughtful analysis of the political situation. So what was *Intro*'s representative doing here at Leeds Motorcycles?

"I'll be frank and not waste your time," Leonard Coxe was saying. "I tried to reach you by phone, but the line was busy, and to be honest, I wanted to see you and talk to you face to face." His pale eyes were busily taking in details of the shop. Cecily saw them glance over the photographs of Art on the back wall. "First, let me say that I was a fan of yours, Mr. Leeds. I covered the Grand Prix race in Italy some years ago when you won the twenty-five-lap short-track event."

Looking as pleased as a boy on Christmas morning, Art Leeds shrugged. "I just got lucky, Mr. Coxe."

"Please—call me 'Leonard.' I hope we can do business together."

"What kind of business?" George asked immediately. "You want to interview Art, is that it? Is *Intro* doing some kind of feature on sports personalities?"

"Not quite, Mr. . . . ? But an interview is what we had in mind." Leonard Coxe turned back to Art, adding, "I understand Ryan Alexander has approached you with an offer. You're going to help him lay the groundwork for a motorcycle tour through New Hampshire, Connecticut, New York State and New Jersey. Am I correct?"

Bewildered, Art looked at George, then at Cecily. "I'm not sure I know what you're talking about."

The man from *Intro* smiled. "Come, Mr. Leeds, don't be coy. We have our sources, and whatever Ryan Alexander does is big news." When Art continued to blink bemusedly, he persisted, "Naturally, you're aware that at twenty-eight he controls not only the nationwide Raya department-store chain, but also this new and highly successful business of his, Ryan A. Tours, Inc."

"'Tours'?" Art echoed feebly.

"The firm has already overseen a fabulously successful hang-gliding adventure over Hawaii, scuba diving off the Bahamas. Ryan Alexander participates in each of his tours, which are exclusive and tremendously expensive." Coxe paused as if for effect. "He's been called every man's envy and every woman's fantasy. When we heard he was going to offer a motorcycle tour in this area, we kept very close tabs on him—and those tabs have led us to you. We're willing to pay absolutely top dollar for an article about your experiences along the trail with Ryan Alexander."

Before her father could speak, Cecily intervened. "What makes you think Leeds Motorcycles accepted Mr. Alexander's offer?"

Leonard Coxe gave her a somewhat pitying look. "Any motorcycle enthusiast would give his right arm to go on such an adventure. And after all, glamour attracts, doesn't it? Not only would an association with someone like Ryan Alexander bring you business, it would also open all kinds of doors for you."

Like the doors of banks, Cecily thought. She refused to meet her father's bewildered eyes and remained silent as Leonard Coxe continued.

"The article we'd want would be a combination of travelogue and introspective account of days spent with Ryan Alexander. He's a fascinating man. Tremendously successful in business, of course, with offices and personal residences in Boston, Chicago, New York and in many parts of Europe. His achievements in sports and his romances with glamorous women have become public domain. But there's a private side to him, as well." Leonard Coxe lifted his well-manicured finger to emphasize the point. "No one knows what makes Ryan Alexander really tick. Men want to know more about him. And women—well each hopes she'll be the one to unlock the deep secrets of Ryan Alexander's soul."

Both Art and George were staring at Leonard Coxe. George's mouth was lightly open. Cecily said, "We'll keep your...angle in mind, Mr. Coxe, but we haven't come to any decision yet about the offer to accompany Ryan Alexander." She took the man from *Intro*'s card, promised to telephone him the moment a decision had been made.

Two days ago she thought she had made that decision. Yet now she wasn't so sure. There was the money, the retainer promised by Ryan, and then this commission from *Intro*. How could she kiss so much money goodbye, when George insisted they were in such trouble? Besides, there was real trouble now that Art knew about Ryan's offer.

Art was saying somewhat plaintively, "What kind of motorcycle tour was he talking about? What's going on, Cecily, or are you in the dark like I am?"

"No, she's not." George was so excited that he seized his mustache with both hands and tugged at it. "Matt told me about the man who was with Cecily at Jedborough. Said his name was Ryan something, that he helped Matt after his accident. Tall, handsome dude, Matt said. That must've been Ryan Alexander."

There was nothing to do but to explain, and as she did so, Cecily watched Art's faded hazel eyes turn young and eager again. "Of course I'll go!" he exclaimed. "Think of all that money, George. Even you should be happy with all that bread coming in!"

George groaned. "You damned old fool, you'd never make it to Conway," he snapped. "Your arthritis, remember?" Art began to argue, but the irascible little man silenced him. "Most mornings you hurt so bad you can hardly stand up. How could you handle yourself along the trail?"

The stricken look on her father's face went to Cecily's heart like a spear. She started to speak, but Art was already shaking his head. "George is right, Ceci," he said quietly. "I guess I always knew, anyway. I'm too old. But there's nothing to stop you from taking my place."

At once George objected. "She's a woman!" he cried. Art rounded on him, wanting to know if Cecily wasn't the best motorcycle mechanic in these parts and a damned good rider.

"I know all that. But—" George cleared his throat uncertainly, rocking back and forth on his heels. "It wouldn't look good," he finally ventured.

"Afraid of what the neighbors would say?" The deep voice seemed to murmur the words in Cecily's ear. As her father and George moved away, still arguing, she automatically picked up her tools to work on Matt Zolichick's injured BMW. Usually work soothed her mind and her heart, but today her concentration didn't hold. It didn't matter that Ryan was "every man's envy and every woman's fantasy." What mattered was that he could be the solution to Leeds Motorcycles' problems. With that kind of financial cushion, so much was possible. And Leonard Coxe was right in saying that association with a man like Ryan Alexander would open new doors to them.

She put down her tools and rested her cheek for a second against the harsh, twisted metal of the BMW. What would it be like to be free of debt and worry—to see Leeds Motorcycles grow into a flourishing business, even to fulfill her dream someday to travel the world with Art? Through Ryan's offer that could become reality.

Behind her, Art had begun to test out a cycle engine—probably the old, wrecked Italian racer he'd bought. With the loud, familiar noises as background, she tried to marshal her thoughts. If she didn't agree to go with Ryan, Art might decide he was fit enough for the trip, after all. She knew him well enough to sense how tempted he was even now. He wasn't strong enough, whereas she was a very good mechanic and a good biker. And with Art's consent, there was nothing to stop her from going, nothing at all.

The roaring sound of the engine behind her seemed to concur. "All I have to do is to telephone him," she told herself, but the words were a mistake. They conjured up a tall, dark-haired man with gray eyes the color of the sun-flecked sea, a broad-shouldered man whose fine lips were curved in a self-assured smile, who even in imagination exuded a force and vitality that made mere men pale by comparison. She shut her eyes as if to rid herself of Ryan's image and spoke firmly. "This would be strictly and purely business."

"Talking to yourself is a bad sign. How long has this been going on?" a deep voice asked from behind her.

Cecily turned so quickly that she felt dizzy. He was no figment of her imagination—he was really there. "What are you doing here?" she demanded.

He was dressed casually in jeans and a Windbreaker over a simple open-collared sport shirt; still he conveyed that aura of wealth. "Sorry if I surprised you, but you looked very preoccupied. I was in the general area and decided to stop by to meet your father—and George. Quite a character, George Zolichick. I like him." His eyes softening, he added, "As for Art, he's still the same man I saw race years ago. One look at my machine, and he couldn't keep his fingers off the controls. He's taken George for a spin around the area."

"'Taken George'?" Cecily couldn't help laughing. She could just imagaine the two men—Art urging Ryan's powerful Electra Glide to greater speeds, and George hanging on and hollering and turning red. Then she sobered. "You're here about the tour."

He nodded, "I hope you've reconsidered. There are other motorcycle mechanics I could approach in New England, but Leeds Motorcycles is still my top choice." He paused. "I didn't bring the tour up, by the way. Your father was the one who spoke about it first, and he seemed anxious that you go instead of him. He seemed to think it would be a lot of fun and an adventure, but you know, of course, that there's another side to the trip. There would be backbreaking work at times, and discomfort, and although we'd stop at hotels and motels along the way, there would be many nights when we'd camp out and rough it. I can't even promise good weather."

His forthright, businesslike manner was reassuring, but she still hesitated. "Supposing we begin the tour, and we mutually decide we can't go on together?"

"The three thousand dollars I mentioned on Sunday would still be yours regardless of whether the decision to quit was mutual or yours alone," he said at once. "I'm not trying to box you in or get you to agree to terms that aren't comfortable to you. This tour is important to me. Its success depends on our working together." He paused and then said quietly, "Yes or no?"

Her heart started to pound. There was no more putting off the decision, and she knew it. She thought of the money and the adventure. She sighed. "Yes. All right—yes. I'll do it."

"Good." The pleasure in his deep tone made something inside her blossom with an unlooked-for warmth; for a moment all the electricity that had sparked between them on Sunday came surging back. Perhaps this was only relief because the decision had been made, but she felt suddenly happy and excited.

"I'll probably live to regret this," she said.

"No, you won't. You'll tell your grandchildren someday that you crossed the White Mountains and the Pine Barrens on a motorcycle, and they'll think you're some old lady." He drew a folded map from the pocket of his Windbreaker and, resting one booted foot on the low workstand, smoothed the map over his kness. "Here's our travel route. On the chance that you could be persuaded, I came prepared."

Leaning closer, she followed the strong, tanned finger pointing to Copley Square in Boston, where the spring motorcycle tour would begin. "For the actual trip, the members of the tour will have flown in some nights before, and on the eve of the trip there'll be a banquet in their honor at the Copley Plaza Hotel, where suites will have been reserved for them. Since we want to duplicate their movements as faithfully as possible, we'll also be starting there, at nine o'clock this Saturday." Sea-gray eyes swung up to meet hers. "You do remember I said we'd have to leave within the week. I have some pressing business commitments, and besides, we want to take advantage of the good weather. Those mountain passes can get pretty cold by mid-October."

Cecily listened as he outlined the route they would take: Route 95 out of Boston, then to 16, which would take them to the beginning of the Kankamagus Highway. They'd stop that night in a picturesque town called Whitwater and then head into Vermont on back trails, many of them challenging and some mildly dangerous. As she listened, she realized why Ryan A. Tours, Inc. was as successful as it was. Ryan's proposed tour was a clever blend of rugged trail adventures and the unexpected luxury of cozy little-known country inns. And, he added, she would need to pack a dress. They would be staying at the Eliott House, a luxurious hotel on the outskirts of Trenton, New Jersey, where Ryan's tour members would enjoy a gala banquet before plunging into the mysterious 650,000-acre forest that made up New Jersey's Pine Barrens.

She had almost been holding her breath as she listened to him. "The Kankamagus—the Pine Barrens—the Kittatiny Mountains," she murmured. The names themselves were magic. It was almost as if she were little again, sitting beside Art with the map of the world between them, dreaming of the trips they would take together.

"Some say that the Kittatiny Mountains are haunted by the spirits of the Lenai Lenape Indians who lived there long ago." Ryan was smiling, but his eyes were thoughtful.

"I hope they don't mind being disturbed by motorcyclists." Cecily realized as she spoke that her excitement came not simply from what he told her, but from her abrupt awareness of his closeness. She could pretend to ignore his powerful, muscular presence, but she couldn't stop breathing, and the scent of him, the clean, vital, masculine fragrance, seemed to encircle and invade. She struggled to find words to counter this seige and bring order to her troubled senses.

"Will you show this map to Art?" she asked. "He'll enjoy hearing about the trip, and he'll probably have many good suggestions."

"I intend to. That's why I'm hiring Leeds Motorcycles in the first place," Ryan agreed. "I'll have my lawyers draw up the terms of our agreement, and I want you and Art to be my guests in Boston when we sign. We can talk over dinner." He held out his hand. "Well, partner, do we have a deal?"

Unthinking, she took his hand, remembered too late, as the cool, firm clasp closed around her fingers, that strange magic accompanied his touch. Shock waves sizzled through her like static electricity, reaching deep into the core of her. Her pulses leaped, and even the coursing of her blood seemed different, as if a wild, sweet honey had taken its place.

Involuntarily she took a step away. Her movement was uncharacteristically awkward, so that she caught her heel against the workstand.

"Careful," he warned, and the hand that still held hers tightened, pulling her forward and away from the danger of falling. She sought to regain her balance, couldn't do it. She fell forward into his arms.

For a moment there was only surprise, and her eyes flew up to meet his. His deep gray gaze expressed neither amusement nor self assurance, but an astonishment that matched her own. Then the surprise changed, became an undefinable, here-now and gone-again emotion as his head bent down toward hers.

Cecily seemed to be reacting in slow motion. Irresistibly, as if pulled back by the weight of her red-gold hair, her head tipped back. Her eyelashes swooped down to shield her from the hot silver of his gaze. And then his mouth touched hers in the lightest of kisses.

It was only a momentary caress. Yet in that second she registered everything. For a heartbeat's time she breathed and tasted and felt him, and each beat of her pulse sent desire through her blood like firebloom. The world around her and everyone in it seemed to disappear, leaving only a stillness that held her and Ryan.

"Are you all right?" There was a quizzical tilt to his eyebrows, and whatever emotion she had seen so briefly in his eyes had gone. He looked as it he were used to having women swooning into his arms. Surely he didn't think she'd planned to trip like that?

Hastily she pulled away from him. There was a roaring in her ears, and she almost shook her head to clear it before she realized that what she heard was Art and George returning on Ryan's Electra Glide. She looked up at him, encountering faint amusement in his smile.

"We haven't even started out yet," he was telling her. "You want to watch your step, partner."

Annoyed at him and even more at herself, she pitched her voice above the oncoming engine. "Don't worry, I intend to."

And where Ryan Alexander was concerned, that was one promise she intended to keep.

3

"BRAKES!" Art called out sharply.

On her knees between Ryan's cycle and her own, Cecily replied, "Check."

"Clutch—Ceci, have you made sure you adjusted those clutch cables?"

She nodded.

"All right, check. Carburetor?"

"I checked the carburetors of both cycles this morning, and Matt's made sure the shocks are at the proper level." Cecily put down her screwdriver and gave her own Sportster a gentle pat. "You're some hunk of machine, do you know that?" she said lovingly.

The gleaming motorcycle seemed to purr. Nearby, Ryan's powerful machine stood emitting the superior aura that came from fine tuning and a careful going-over at the hands of masters. "Have you checked the CBs?" Art was asking. "You're leaving tomorrow, don't forget, and you have to communicate with each other on the road."

"The CBs are fine." Cecily got up off her knees and walked over to the rickety chair Art had dragged out near the workstand. Leaning down, she gave him an affectionate hug. "Are *you* okay?"

He patted her cheek, sighing. "I keep telling myself you'll be fine. Even George agrees."

She ruffled what was left of his gray hair. "You're not to worry. I'll be having the time of my life. When I come home I'll tell you all about it, and we'll celebrate. We'll take George and Edna and Matt to Jimmy's Harborside and have lobster on all the money I'll be raking in. I'll be back before you know it."

Art's face brightened and then fell. "Three weeks." He spoke gloomily. "Shouldn't you and Ryan go over everything this evening? A last-minute check on the cycles and the tools you're going to take before you hit the road?"

"Ryan's a busy man. That's why he hired us."

Art frowned. "You've been busy, too, too busy to rub two thoughts together."

It was true. On Wednesday Cecily and Art had driven into Boston to sign a formal contract between Leeds Motorcycles and Ryan A. Tours, Inc. The signing had taken place in Ryan's sumptuous executive office, which took up an entire floor of the John Hancock Building.

The difference between their small shop and that opulent setting, with Aubusson rugs and glove-soft leather furniture, had made her feel a little like a poor relation, but Ryan had seemed unaware of her discomfort. He had been completely businesslike as they discussed the tour details over dinner at the elegant Maison de Robert. He had as good as told her that for the rest of the week she was on her own. Though she was to charge all she needed to his company, readying his motorcycle and her own Sportster for the trip, gathering needed tools and equipment was her responsibility. He in turn would take care of all the camping gear for the days and nights they would spend in the outdoors.

After that meeting she hadn't seen him; though they communicated regularly by telephone, their conversations revolved around the business of getting ready by Saturday. Fortunately, Matt Zolichick helped by chasing down parts and putting in routine maintenance on other cycles that came in. He also volunteered to work with Art until he had to return to U of Mass later in September.

As Art said, she'd been too busy to think much, and she liked it that way. While concentrating on getting ready for the trip, she'd put other considerations back into focus. Now she felt firmly in control. Though she had to admit to a certain attraction between her and Ryan, this trip was purely business for both of them. As he'd told her, it was important to him, and he'd do his best to work with her. She was going to see that they kept things that way.

"I'd better phone Ryan's office and leave word that we're all clear at this end," she told Art. "I'm going to bed early tonight, and you'd better, too. You have to drive me into Boston tomorrow, early."

As she spoke the phone began to shrill. "That's probably Ryan now," Art said.

There was, Cecily told herself, a perfectly good explanation for the involuntary leap of her pulse. It stemmed from the excitement of the adventure that was to begin tomorrow. Yet when she took up the receiver, a familiar tenor voice deflated her. "Ms Leeds? Leonard Coxe here. Do you remember me?"

Guiltily Cecily realized she'd forgotten about him and his offer. "Mr. Coxe—of course," she began apologetically. "There's just been so much going on."

Clicking his tongue, the man from *Intro* smoothed things over. "That's quite understandable, Ms Leeds.

If I were going off on an exciting tour with Ryan Alexander, I probably wouldn't know my knee from my elbow about now. I don't want to harry you, of course, but now that you've accepted Ryan A. Tours's offer, could we talk about *Intro*'s proposition again?"

Cecily hesitated. "As Mr. Alexander's employee, I owe him a certain loyalty. I can't do anything against his wishes. I remember your saying that he was a very private person, Mr. Coxe. If he doesn't want a personal article written about him, I couldn't write it."

"Of course not." Leonard Coxe's tone dropped to an even more cajoling smoothness. "I assure you we're not the kind of magazine that specializes in exposés or sensational news stories. What we suggest is that you take some notes—you know, of what Ryan Alexander says, how he thinks, what he does on the tour—and give us a profile. This kind of candid article would be worth quite a bit to us." He named a sum that made her eyes snap wide open. Ryan Alexander's character was worth that much?

Even so, she still held back. "I can take a few notes...that won't do any harm," she said slowly. "But after I write the article I'd have to run it by him first. And if he doesn't like it—that's the end." She paused and added with a chuckle, "I doubt if he'd like it, Mr. Coxe. I'm handier with a wrench and screwdriver than I am with a pen."

Expecting argument, she was surprised by his enthusiastic response. "That's settled, then," he said jovially. "Don't worry about not being a success, Cecily—I may call you Cecily—I'm sure anything you do is bound to please Ryan Alexander."

SATURDAY DAWNED blue and gold, a perfect day with the gentle warmth of New England Septembers. Art drove Cecily and her motorcycle in their old van, interspersing silence with advice. He seemed to have forgotton he'd called her an expert mechanic—he gave her long lectures on maintenance jobs she could do in her sleep. She was grateful when at last they reached Boston and Copley Square, but as they pulled up to the Copley Plaza Hotel, from which the tour was to depart, Art groaned.

"Good grief!" he exclaimed. "Look at the press and the TV cameras. You'd think the president was coming."

She had known Ryan would arrange for the media to be present, but she hadn't expected so much coverage, and as she gazed at members of the press, representatives of local and national magazines, TV news cameras all poised and ready, she realized the truth of what Leonard Coxe had said. Whatever Ryan Alexander did was news.

Cecily spotted him almost at once. He was talking to several news people, his broad wedge of shoulders and his height making him unmistakable. She had to admit that if he was indeed every man's envy and the fantasy of most women, he was certainly dressed for the part. The black leather riding suit fit his powerful form like a glove. In it he exuded both masculinity and strength. When he turned, sunlight glinted off his hair, creating blue highlights, and shone over the restless eagerness on his face.

"You made good time—I didn't expect you for another half-hour." Striding over to them, he shook hands with Art while his eyes went quickly to her.

She knew from his smile of satisfaction that he found her good to look at, and that the color of the apple-green scarf she wore tucked into her dark leathers—a bon-voyage gift from the Zolichicks—matched her eyes. The green brought out the creamy sheen of her skin and enhanced the fiery highlights in her hair.

"You look very photogenic and charming and efficient," he told her. "The press is here to give my firm's spring offering as much publicity as it wants. You wouldn't mind answering a few questions, would you?"

The questions were mostly predictable. "Cecily, how do you feel about being a woman in a traditional man's profession?"

"How did it feel growing up as Art Leeds's daughter?"

"Are you looking foward to three weeks on the road with Ryan Alexander?"

Then came the picture taking. Obediently Cecily straddled her motorcycle, smiled, waved, posed with Ryan and then with Art. As they posed together, Art managed to slip in some more advice.

"I'm not worried about your riding—you're the best. Just be sure to keep that CB plugged into your belt so that you can communicate with Ryan. And ride carefully. Don't take chances." To Ryan, who came up to them, Art added, "Take care of Cecily, will you? She's special to me."

Ryan nodded gravely. I'll do my best, but I have a feeling Cecily will be taking care of me."

There were unabashed tears in Art's eyes, and Cecily felt a lump in her throat. How many times, she wondered, had this scene been played in reverse? She'd seen Art off on tour or on the race circuit so many times. She had watched him fly away or drive or ride away with her heart in her mouth and prayed for his safe return. Now she knew how he felt. She gave him a big hug after which he muttered, deadpan, "Don't go spitting against the wind, Ceci."

She was still grinning when she followed Ryan to her machine and let him ceremoniously hand her onto the saddle for the benefit of the recording cameras. He then mounted his Electra Glide.

As they accelerated away, the smooth, strong power of their machines blending in a moment of almost total harmony, she could hear behind her the babble of the press and Art's shouts of encouragement. She carried his goodbyes with her as they wove in and out of Boston's weekend traffic, then took 95 out of the city.

Once away from Boston, Cecily tipped back her head and drew it all in, the golden air, the beloved and familiar scent of leather, wind, dust and exhaust, and felt exhilaration run through her like a cool draught of wine. They were on their way.

She and Ryan continued along 95 for the better part of two hours. Then, as the highway forked into Route 16, he suggested over the CB, "Do you want to stretch your legs and take a breather? There's a rest area about a mile ahead."

She agreed that was a good idea, and when they had reached the rest area, she was grateful for the chance to bend and stretch. Ryan unpacked a stainless-steel thermos of coffee from his saddlebags. They shared the sweet dark liquid. "It must be the road," she told him. "I've rarely had coffee this good."

His smile was friendly. "Be careful, Cecily. The fresh air can go to your head."

She pushed her goggles up to look up at him. "You're talking to Art Leeds's daughter, remember? I know all about riding going to your head."

"I wish he could have come along, too," Ryan agreed, suddenly serious. "It must be hard for him to be left behind."

The caring in his voice brought a warmth that didn't jibe with the resolutions she'd made to hold this man at arm's length. "Art gets emotional at times—that's the way he is," she said as lightly as she could.

"He's a smart man, then." She looked at Ryan surprised, at which he shrugged those broad shoulders. "He's honest enough to show his feelings. Not many people can do that. It shows strength."

Art, strong? She'd always seen him as the somewhat impractical dreamer, the idealist George Zolichick was always complaining about. "He did manage to keep the family together after mom died," she said slowly, as if following a new thought. "He can do dumb things, but when push comes to shove, he's right there. I remember one time in school when I was in a play..."

Her words trailed off. Surely Ryan wasn't interested in her reminiscences. But the silver-gray eyes were keen and intent. "Go on," he said as she slowed down.

Diffidently she kicked at the ground with the toe of her boot. "I'd fought for the lead—Laura in the *Glass Menagerie*—and I'd made it. Then we realized the play was in March, and that Art was going to race at Daytona. I knew how important Daytona was to Art, so I said nothing about the play. I guess he knew how I felt though."

"And he didn't race?"

She laughed. "He raced, all right, but he flew back to see my play—between races. He didn't tell me. On opening night there he was sitting right in the front row, grinning at me and giving me the high sign." She shook her head at the memory. "George nearly had apoplexy when he heard how much the plane fare cost, but right then I didn't care."

"I suppose you know you're both pretty lucky." The sudden change in his deep tone made her look up but nothing showed on his face. Abruptly he recapped the thermos and replaced it, adding, "And if we're lucky we might outrun that."

"What?" But her eyes were already following his pointing finger, and she caught her breath in surprise.

Where had those clouds come from? Instead of blue skies, a solid bank of gray was rolling rapidly toward them. A low, cool breeze had also begun to keen, and she didn't like the feel of it. Neither did Ryan. "It's going to rain pretty soon," he said. "It'll hit us before we make it over the Kankamagus." He adjusted his helmet. "Let's go."

The second stage of their journey was not as pleasant as the first. The gloom of the skies increased, while the winds unmistakably carried the threat of rain. As they rode into the small town of Chocorua, Ryan halted his motorcycle and glanced skyward again. "We've got two options. We can stay here and wait it out, or push over the Kankamagus toward Whitwater."

This was the first time he was asking her opinion, and she took a moment to think the decision through. "It seems to me that if your tour wouldn't stop because of rain, neither should we."

He nodded, but his somber looks didn't lighten. "You're right, but I don't care for the thought of coming down those curves along the Kankamagus in the rain. Let's move."

But there was only so much speed that could be safely mustered, and they weren't halfway to the top of the winding road when it began to drizzle. Stopping to pull ponchos out of their saddlebags, they eyed the gorge below. It was shrouded in gray, the cliff side of the twisted road obscured by deep cottony swatches of fog. And the mist wasn't the main problem. As they rode higher, the winds increased in velocity. Thunder began to growl in the distance.

Hardly the ideal day for a ride in the country. Grimly Cecily concentrated on the road surface. Art had taught her, years ago, to pay strict attention to the condition of the road. It was never, he had often lectured her, the road's fault when a rider skidded; the rider's lack of attention was the culprit....

She gasped as a fork of lightning dazzled the gloom ahead of her; almost simultaneously thunder boomed. As if that were some sort of signal, rain began to fall. Huge, seemingly vengeful drops smashed down on them, and the wind turned vicious. As they came to a curve in the road, a wicked crosswind caught them, rocking even Ryan's sturdy Harley Low Rider and causing Cecily's lighter motorcycle to teeter dangerously.

She struggled to control her machine, but as she downshifted, the front wheel of her cycle jolted violently. The next moment she found herself riding into a rain-filled pothole, with no way to escape the wave of water that was drifting toward her. As she tried to compensate by steering away from the wave, she heard Ryan's crisp command over the CB.

"Left—bear left, Cecily. The ground's firm on the left."

Automatically, she obeyed, revving the engine to stop water from entering the exhaust pipes. Thunder roared and crashed around them again as she bounced hard on the far side of the pothole and emerged on level ground once more. "Are you all right?" Ryan demanded. "That was some hole in the ground."

She nodded. "My fault for not seeing it." The CB was crackling loudly with static, but she saw him shake his head.

"Not your fault. The weather—" The rest of his sentence was doused by more static and the roar of wind as another streak of lightning tore open the sky just above them. When the accompanying thunder had splintered away, she caught the one word, "Shelter."

Where could they find shelter out here? She glanced to her right and saw trees masking the sheer sides of the misty cliff. To the left, there loomed a dark mountain with a ski run showing like a white scar down its face. "Over there!" she heard him call as he turned his motorcycle toward the mountain.

Then Cecily saw what he was heading for. There was a cluster of small, dark buildings at the base of the mountain, probably ski chalets closed for the season. Grateful that Ryan's keen eyesight had picked them out in this gloom, she followed him as he veered off the highway, across ground that was rutted and covered with low-growing vegetation. Standing upright on her footrests, she urged her cycle as swiftly as possible toward the hoped-for shelter. The torrent of rain, the thunder, the roaring wind around her—she was blinded and deafened. Then they were on a gravel path circling toward the closest of the buildings.

It looked to be some kind of shed, probably used to house skis and equipment during the season. Thankfully she pulled up beside Ryan's Electra Glide and dismounted. As she did so, her foot twisted in treacherous, slick mud.

Though her involuntary gasp of pain had been muffled, he still heard her. "What is it? Are you hurt?" Ryan asked.

"I'm all right. Just help me get my motorcycle out of the rain. . . ."

His cooperation was swift and efficient, and her respect for him as a working partner grew. He seemed to intuit what needed to be done, and he certainly wasn't afraid of hard work. When they'd managed to shelter their motorcycles, he turned to her. "Your foot's bothering you, isn't it? Lean on me."

Without waiting for her reply, he wrapped an arm around her shoulders and half walked, half carried her to shelter. She caught her breath in a reaction that had nothing to do with the pain in her foot. Even at such a moment, she reacted to the hard pressure of his lean side, the musculature of hip and thigh.

He looked down at her in concern. "We won't get far if you've hurt your foot badly. I'd better have a look."

Efficiently he helped her to remove her poncho, after which he assisted her to a corner of the hut and knelt down in front of her. As she struggled to take off her boot, she was acutely aware of his nearness. Muscle and sinew rippled like silk under the taut black leather of his riding gear, and the thought came to her that he looked as if he was almost naked.

"Let me see." He caught her foot in his hands once she'd removed boot and sock, and the warmth of his fingers on her cold skin was more disturbing than the pain that followed his moving her foot gently. "Does that hurt?"

"A little, but I don't think it's even a sprain. I should have looked where I was stepping before I put my weight down. It'll be all right, Ryan, really. Once we get to Whitwater I'll soak and bind it."

"Why wait?" He got to his feet, the movement again emphasizing his powerful physique, and strode over to his motorcycle. From the saddlebags he removed a roll of athletic bandage and tape; with this he expertly bound her ankle. She felt physical relief almost immediately, but his prolonged nearness caused a different unease. His sleek, wet head, bowed so intimately close to her, brought her senses to tingling life. She found herself imagining the feel of that crisp darkness against her fingers, and caught her breath, only to be filled with the scent of him. That strong, clean male fragrance rose over the smells of rain and wet earth and crushed grass.

"Now, try it," he was saying.

Glad to be doing something, Cecily eased her weight onto her hurt foot and felt only a twinge of pain. "You sure know how to take care of a sprain."

"I've had practice. Can you believe I bound up someone else's ankle around here nearly twenty years ago? In a storm very much like this one, as a matter of fact."

Outside the rain still roared down, and the thunder growled. "What happened to this friend of yours?"

He sank beside her on the wooden floor of the hut. "It started out as an adventure. My pal Jordan—his folks had a cottage next to our summer place in the White Mountains—and I decided to try out our new five-speed bikes, and we got lost. Then a summer storm hit, and we were both pertified. Luckily I found shelter...."

"As you did today," she murmued. They were so close, that when he gestured their shoulders touched. She wanted to shift a little away, but at the same time she didn't want to move. A strange languor filled her, a weakness that didn't result from fatigue.

Ryan nodded, memory softening his face. For a moment he looked young and vulnerable. The idea surprised her. Now how could someone like Ryan Alexander ever be vulnerable?

He was saying, "Jordan sprained his foot, so that I had to tear up my shirt and make a bandage. We couldn't peddle back to our house, and the storm went on and on—it was evening before Jordan's folks found us."

"They must have been frantic!"

"They were. His mother was an all-right lady, though. She fed us and gave us a hot bath and told me that with my talents I could either be a doctor or an explorer."

She laughed. "I'll bet your own mother had a few things to say, too."

"She didn't know about it. She was in Europe at the time—on her third honeymoon, I think." He cogitated for a moment before nodding. "Yes, that was when she was married to Kirk Woode, the banker. And dad was in New York planning the takeover of an important company. Of course, the housekeeper at their summer place was fit to be tied."

She said, "Oh."

Dark eyebrows slanted up quizzically. "Believe me, I could take care of myself." His deep voice was strong and assured. "My parents taught me self-reliance early. I've always believed that the only person you can completely rely on is yourself. It makes life simpler."

She thought of dear, impulsive Art and lovable, grumbling George. And kind Edna and the memories she'd always have of her beautiful mother. They were her family, the people without whom her life would not, could not, be rich or happy. "It's lonely at the top...." The old saying filtered through her mind, and as she looked up at Ryan uncertainly, she saw that again his eyes were shadowed.

Before she could react or even think, a crack of lightning seared down. This time it hit almost right on top of them. Cecily could smell and even taste ozone, while the whole hut rocked with the accompanying thunder. She moved involuntarily, turning to the only place of safety she could think of—his arms.

For a second she clung to him, grateful for the warm, solid strength of his body. Then she managed a shaky chuckle. "That was too close."

Whatever else she had meant to say faded from her mind as her eyes met his. The shadow was still there, but it had changed, had softened his features and made his firm mouth grow tender.

"Ryan..." she whispered, and then his mouth was on hers.

HIS LIPS WERE WARM and tasted sweet. There was a magic in them that made the blood course through her until she felt giddy. She was surrounded by the clean scent of after-shave and a vibrant masculinity that was distinctively his, and as she breathed and tasted of him, she felt the hard strength of his arms. Some instinct of self-preservation, now buried deep under rivulets of pleasure, told her she had to pull away from him. Yet, she couldn't move. Sensations seemed to be imploding softly, filling her with undulating shock waves. She didn't want to pull away from him. She wanted to get closer.

Intuiting her desire, Ryan drew her nearer with one arm, while his other rose to cradle her head. Sensitive fingers stroked her nape and smoothed the wet silk of her hair. At the same time his mouth was also stroking, his tongue brushing the periphery of her lips. Under its insistence, they parted to his bold invasion.

"Cecily." The sound of his deep voice sighing her name was another caress. She reached up to feel the crisp, dark hairs under her fingers and then traced the hard line of his jaw. He turned his mouth slightly to brush her fingertips with his mouth before seeking her lips again.

The tips of their tongues touched, their breath mingling. She arched her back against his supporting hand, no longer knowing where her softness ended and where his hardness began. Her pulses sang and roared in her ears, so that she couldn't even hear the storm when his hand left her waist and stroked down over her hip and then upward over the slenderness of her waist and ribs. Lightly, so as to be almost no touch at all, his fingers and palm brushed the curve of her breast. Once...twice. She murmured against his mouth and nestled closer to him, seeking once more that knowing, delicate caress.

The flash of pain caught her by surprise; Cecily gasped. The sound was muted against his mouth, but she felt his arms tense and then loosen around her. "What is it?"

Without the pressure of his arms around her, she felt bereft. Instinctively she moved closer to him, and again there was pain, jabbing up from her ankle, through her leg. This time it served to clear her mind.

"Your ankle?" he was asking. When she nodded, he let go of her completely so that he could examine her foot, frowning with concern as he rechecked her bandage. "You shouldn't ride any farther today with that ankle. We'll ride into Whitwater tandem, get someone to come out and tow your bike in."

"You mean, leave my motorcycle here? You've got to be joking, Ryan. I can't do that."

"Motorcycles can be replaced, but it would be hard to find another Cecily Leeds." He patted her foot gently. "Besides, I don't want to jeopardize this trip in any way."

His words jolted her back to full awareness. She'd forgotten how differently they looked at the world. To Ryan a fully dressed Harley was something that could be acquired with the mere signing of a check. Her mind flitted back to how she had scrimped to buy her motorcycle, how she and Art had worked on the cycle and checked it. And loved it—that most of all.

"I promise I won't cave in on you and ruin things," she told him. "I can ride very well, and I'll be fine by tomorrow. Art made sure I packed a special ointment he has for bruises and sprains. I don't know what's in it, but it always works."

"Are you sure?" He took both her hands in his. "There's no need to tough it out, Cecily."

The strong, sure clasp was disturbing. It reminded her of another thing she'd forgotten, her decision to keep this trip on a strictly professional level. A decision that was wavering again under his direct gaze and his touch. "Please don't worry," she said with all the firmness she could muster. "I really am pretty tough."

He grinned. "Even if thunder scares you?"

"That thunderclap came so suddenly it startled me." His grin widened, and she added with spirit, "Don't tell me you weren't as surprised as I was."

"In more ways than one." Lifting her hands, he dropped a light kiss on the knuckles before letting them go. "All right, then, partner. If you're sure, we'll wait a little while longer and then ride into Whitwater together. The rain should ease up soon."

He got up to look out at the still-dripping sky, and Cecily was grateful for the distance between them. She drew a deep, bracing breath and determinedly ignored Ryan's insidious after-shave clinging to the air. Once more she reminded herself that they were colleagues who had been startled by that sudden blast of thunder. That was all that had happened, and the sooner the incident was forgotten, the better.

"Can you tell me about Whitwater?" she asked briskly. "You've said it's a picturesque town. Is there anything else I should know?"

"Mainly that the town fathers aren't convinced that Ryan A. Tours is such a good idea."

She was surprised. "I thought that after the publicity you've received from your other tours, any town would be delighted to host your clients. Ryan A. Tours has got to be a name that will bring a lot of tourist business to Whitwater."

He turned to face her, his smile rueful. "Whitwater is a small, feisty Yankee town. It always votes down any kind of industry that will change it from the bedroom community it is, and it doesn't like tourists much, either. I imagine the town fathers hit the roof when they got my letter of inquiry about the tour. Jed Alcott, one of the selectmen, wrote back politely that they weren't interested, but that they'd meet with me if I insisted."

"Then why not go somewhere else?" she asked practically.

"Whitwater is ideal for my purposes. It's off the beaten track, has fine scenery, a first-class inn." Ryan shook his head firmly. "No. It's up to me to get Whitwater to welcome us in the spring like VIPs. I can be persuasive when I want to be."

A ripple of desire, still at large and still dangerous, quivered and set off a chain reaction. Slow, sensuous ripples began to multiply and undulate through her. Quickly, she looked away from him. "I'm sure you can, but maybe persuasion won't work in Whitwater."

"We'll see," He held out a hand to her. "It's starting to clear. If you're sure about that ankle, we'd better get going before it stiffens up on you."

It had already gone stiff, and throbbed with pain as Cecily gingerly drew on her boot, but she tried to ignore it as they rode down the pass. It was still drizzling; the fog was thick, and as they rode in their usual staggered position, Ryan leading, she hoped fervently that Art's ointment would work. Art—suddenly she missed him and wished he *were* beside her.

"How are you holding up?" Ryan's voice asked inside her helmet, and she replied in a sturdy, cheerful tone.

"You're a good trooper," he said then. "If I know anything about ankle injuries, yours is on fire right now. Luckily, Whitwater is just a few miles down the road."

The caring in his voice dispersed her moment of loneliness. "I hope your tour doesn't have to contend with this kind of weather."

"My clients will know how to handle themselves. Most of the response I've got has been from VIPs who own their own machines and have years of riding experience."

As he spoke, she saw something loom up in the fog immediately ahead of them. For a moment she had the horrified thought that someone had built a house in the middle of the road. Then the sound of running water made her realize they were crossing a covered bridge. Wood bumped and rattled under their wheels...and then they seemed to be riding into another world as the road narrowed and led through an avenue of tall trees that glowed green and yellow and even scarlet through the mist.

"It's like looking at jewels through water," she exclaimed, awed by the subdued beauty around her.

"Well put. I should get you to write my copy for the tour. The river's called Mad Turkey River, by the way." She couldn't help laughing, and he added, "Don't be so disrespectful, Ms Leeds. There used to be turkeys in the area, and this river gets quite frisky around the spring thaw. Apparently there's a lot of underground water hereabouts, and it feeds into this waterway."

Obviously, Ryan had done his homework; she was impressed by his knowledge as he continued to tell her about the town. The handsome waterwheel they passed had been built during the depression. Farther along, there was an old-fashioned swimming hole and a spot where it seemed the trout nearly lunged upward to catch the hooks in their mouths. "You might try the trout almondine at the Whitwater Inn tonight," he added as they crested a small slope in the road.

And there below them was the inn. It looked as if it had been lifted out of the page of a history book. Built from dark weathered wood, gabled and wrapped in mist and surrounded by tall oaks and maples, it was impressive, yet somehow welcoming. By mutual accord they stopped to admire the sight.

"I feel as if we've just stepped back in time," Cecily said.

Ryan nodded. "I know my clients will have that same reaction. I'm counting on The Whitwater to take them out of the real, workday world and create the right ambience for the tour." His voice deepened with satisfaction. "The outside of the inn is a couple of hundred years old, but everything inside is supposed to be modern and luxurious. Besides, I'm told they make the best dry martinis this side of the Mason Dixon line."

She couldn't help thinking of the nondescript motels Art had stayed in during his racing days. "Nothing but the best for Ryan A. Tours," she murmured.

He beamed down at her. "Exactly right. My clients pay a lot of money, and they're entitled to the best we can find on this trailblazing trip." He added softly, "There's no law against enjoying yourself."

His mellow voice recalled the strength of his arms, the warmth of his kiss. To counter that memory, Cecily spoke almost sharply. "Right now I'm here to do a job and not to enjoy myself."

He began to laugh.

"What's so funny?" she demanded.

"You and the Puritan work ethic. You should get on fine with Jed Alcott and the town fathers." As he rode away toward the inn, she could hear him chuckling over the CB.

She caught up to him in the inn's surprisingly modern parking lot some minutes later, and maintained a dignified silence as they went through the heavy wooden doors. Here the staff of the inn greeted them with an enthusiasm that was almost effusive, while the innkeeper, a stout, elderly man who looked as if he'd be more at home in knee breeches and homespun instead of his three-piece suit, said the silver and blue rooms had been prepared for Mr. Alexander and his associate.

"The rooms are the finest in the house. I trust everything will be satisfactory, Mr. Alexander." At a snap of his fingers, a bellhop appeared to take their baggage. "If there's anything we can do—anything at all—please let us know."

So the Whitwater Inn, at least, desired Ryan A. Tours' business. Ryan stayed behind to talk to the innkeeper, leaving Cecily to look around her with pleasure as she followed the bellhop up polished wooden stairs. The inn was decorated with fine Chippendale and period furniture, while bowls of autumn flowers glowed like sunbursts under portraits in antique frames heavy with gold. Apparently she and Ryan weren't the only ones who admired the inn. In the sitting room beyond, she could see several guests.

"It seems like a busy time of year for you," she said to the man who was carrying her bags up the stairs.

He nodded. "The dowsers' convention is meeting here." Noting the curious expression on Cecily's face, he asked, "Are you familiar with dowsing?"

"I think so. Don't dowsers hold a forked stick over the ground until it dips to show you've reached underground water?"

"That's what they do, ma'am. For some reason, Whitwater's known as one of the best places for dowsing in these parts, so that every fall folks come from all over. Even Jed Alcott, one of our eldest selectmen, takes part in the dowsing. He's even organized a dowsing demonstration tomorrow on the town green." He paused to push open a door, adding that he hoped she would be comfortable in the Blue Room.

The bellhop needn't have been so humble, for the room oozed with comfort. Everything from the carefully braided blue rugs to the hand-painted blue wallpaper and the sky-blue canopy of the plush four-poster had been selected for luxury. Pastel muslin curtains framed a window that looked out over the misty curl of the river, and beside that window a periwinkle couch practically begged Cecily to sink into it and rest.

She looked at it guiltily. She really should unpack. She should change out of her damp clothes and rub Art's ointment on her throbbing ankle. And she really had to telephone Art so that he and the Zolichicks would quit worrying. Cecily looked hard at the contents of her saddlebags, then at the phone and then at the inviting blue couch. She plopped down onto the couch and sighed as the soft cushions cradled her.

"And you're the woman who doesn't mix business with pleasure." Her eyes flew open to find Ryan standing in the doorway, watching her. He clicked his tongue and shook his head reproachfully, but there was so much amusement in his eyes that she couldn't hold back a smile. "You should shut your door before you decide to goof off on the job."

Ruefully she nodded, and started to get to her feet, wincing involuntarily as her bad foot hit the ground. The laughter left his face at once. "Stay put," he said quickly.

Shutting the door behind him, he strode over to where she sat, pushed what was no doubt a priceless antique hassock into place and sat down before her. But as he began to undo her boots, she protested. "Nobody," she told him indignantly, "has helped me with my boots since I was four. I'm fine, I tell you."

He ignored her. Carefully, he eased the boot off her hurt foot and frowned at her moan of relief. "That needs to be looked after, Cecily." She told him she had meant to do just that, and he took the hurt ankle in his big hand. His touch was gentle. "If there's even the slightest pain tomorrow, we'll stay on another day. I want you to get a good rest."

Rest was the furthest thing from her mind. Her senses were all awake, alive at Ryan's nearness. The Blue Room seemed suddenly small, blatantly feminine in contrast to his masculinity; the air was alive with his distinctive scent. The tingle that had started in her ankle and was spreading throughout her body had nothing to do with the sprain.

"Art's ointment will work," she insisted.

"Need any help with it?" His murmur was inviting, and there was a glint in his gray eyes. "Remember, I've had experience, and your ankle is important to me." He smiled as she shook her head. "Suit yourself."

"You'll see tomorrow. I'll be able to join the dowsers." His eyebrows rose in question, and she explained about the dowsers' convention. "Since there are enthusiasts among the town fathers, maybe we should take a look, too," she added lightly.

To her surprise he took her seriously. "You could be right." He seemed preoccupied for a moment, and then he reached out and gave her knee a pat. The gesture was absentminded. "That could be the answer to a lot of things."

"I wish I knew what you were talking about," she said. As if in answer, he reached out and caught her hand, his clasp light but firm, his thumb stroking across her knuckles and fingers. The small caress seemed to bring back those few moments in the rain, for treacherous honey was spilling into her veins. He turned her hand over and brushed the palm with a kiss. She didn't have the strength of character to pull it away.

When he spoke his tone was brisk. "Perhaps you'd rather have some dinner sent up to your room? You'll need to bathe and rest." He gave the hand he held another small kiss and then swung to his feet, at which point she realized she'd been holding her breath. She let it out very slowly. "After all," he was saying softly, "I want you in top shape for tomorrow. Ryan A. Tours is counting on you."

THE NEXT DAY dawned clear and beautiful, as crisp as a shiny new apple, full of bird song and blue skies scattered with fair-weather clouds. Better still, Cecily found that beyond a trace of tenderness, her ankle felt whole and healed.

"It's Art's miracle ointment," she said to a disbelieving Ryan. "He won't tell me what's in it—tongue of adder and toe of toad, for all I know—but it works."

"He should patent and sell it." Ryan spoke feelingly. "If you're really all right, I'd like you to ride down to the town green with me."

There was nothing in the inflection of his voice, no change in the steady gray eyes; nevertheless she sensed his excitement. "You're really going to the dowsing demonstration? I didn't know you were interested."

"Supposing I told you I've cherished a lifelong dream to throw off the cares of the world and go wandering around the world with a forked stick in my hands?"

"A forked tongue is more likely," she retorted, and he smiled sunnily at her. He looked, she thought, far more like a man on vacation than someone on business. His attire of chinos and a sweater pulled over a shirt added to that impression. Unlike her own modest beige slacks and pullover, however, she assumed his sweater was made of imported cashmere, the trousers superbly tailored, the shirt custom-made. "I'd have thought you'd be more interested in psyching out the town fathers for your meeting tomorrow than in watching them walk around the town green," she said as they left the hotel and walked to the inn's parking lot.

He shrugged. "Sometimes it helps to get a feel for the town before talking business. I've researched Whitwater, but I haven't really walked around in it or talked to the people. There'll be a crowd at the dowsing demonstration, and I might meet someone or learn something useful."

It made sense, Cecily had to admit. She saw, as well, that most of Whitwater had turned out to see the dowsers do their thing. The large Sunday crowd had gathered around a group of slow-walking figures who were crossing the broad, grassy rectangle that lay between the white-spired church and an ancient town hall. There were cars, bikes, even a few reporters covering the event.

"This is probably more excitement than Whitwater sees all year," Ryan commented as he escorted Cecily forward until they were standing on the edge of the green. He turned to a thickset elderly man in a tweed sport coat who was standing beside them. "Fine day for all this," he ventured.

The man glanced at Ryan, then away. "E-yup," he grated.

It wasn't what could be called an encouraging reply, but Ryan continued to be friendly. "Dowsing fascinates me, because there's no explanation for it. Besides, there's that study they just completed at Harding College in Denver. Have you heard about it, Cecily?"

She shook her head. "A study on dowsing, you mean?"

"Absolutely. One of the professors at Harding buried a container of water and had student volunteers walk the area with dowsing rods. The idea was to see whether the rods dipped in the vicinity of the buried water."

The old gentleman beside them was exhibiting signs of curiosity. He half turned to Ryan, and his lips twitched soundlessly as Cecily asked what had happened.

"Charts showed that nearly all the dowsing rods dipped near the hidden water." Ryan turned to the elderly man in the tweed coat. "Are you familiar with that study, sir?"

There was no reason for tension, but Cecily felt it as the elderly stranger stared at Ryan. Old eyes narrowed before he nodded grudgingly. "Read about it. Strange that you should have, though. You're Ryan Alexander—right?" Ryan nodded. "Heard you'd roared into town on your big motorcycle," he added dourly, "but I didn't expect to see you at our small-town dowsing demonstration."

Ryan's voice was quiet, serious. "I've always believed water is our planet's most important resource."

"Resource, hell. A fat lot your industrialists care about resources." The old gentleman almost snorted the words. "Many of your father's companies—his chemical companies, for instance—are always in trouble with the Environmental Protection Agency. You haven't forgotten that he was recently fined for dumping waste in West Virginia, have you?"

Ryan hesitated as if thinking through his answer, but Cecily suddenly realized he was only doing this for effect. Not only did he have the answer down pat, but Ryan had also written and produced this entire scenario. More than that, he'd made sure this meeting would come about in just this way.

Ryan was saying, "I believe the old days are gone. By trying to hold on too hard to the past, we'll lose the future. Still, I don't see eye to eye with my father on many things, and his attitude toward the environment was one of the reasons I left Alexander Industries. Some kinds of progress are too damned expensive, Mr. Alcott."

The old man grunted. "Knew who I was all the time, didn't you? And I suppose you're saying that by trying to keep Whitwater like it is, I'm behind the times." For a moment the Whitwater selectman stood frowning. And then, unexpectedly, he held out a hand. "Are you really interested in dowsing, or was that a ploy to soften me up?"

"Not at all. Ms Leeds—Cecily, here—is really interested." As Jed Alcott's eyes swung in her direction, the younger man added, "In fact, Cecily was the one to suggest we come by and watch you experts in operation."

Ryan's voice didn't change, but she read the look in his eyes as clearly as if he'd spoken. His words were her cue. Now she was to charm Jed Alcott with her supposed interest in dowsing. Irritation stung her. Why couldn't Ryan have been up-front with her, explained what he was up to? She was his associate, after all.

"That so, young lady?" Jed Alcott was demanding. "Here, Alan—young lady wants to give the dowsing rod a chance. Pass one over. Now it's easy. You just hold on here and here."

There was no graceful way to retreat. Uncertainly Cecily took hold of the forked stick and stepped forward onto the green. "Is this right?" she asked, and Jed Alcott actually smiled at her as he fell into step beside her.

"Don't hold on so tight now. Let the rod work for you." He paused. "I suppose you know how I feel about a bike tour coming here. We don't want rowdy motorcyclists banging through our town, messing things up." Jed pauded, and his voice turned slightly sheepish. "I pictured your boss as one of those rich guys who never did a day's work. Someone who'd come down here and wave dollar bills in our faces and tell us how to run things in Whitwater. But he's not like that."

His last sentence turned itself around into a question, and Cecily stifled her growing irritation at Ryan's strategy. As she'd told Leonard Coxe in Boston, she owed Ryan A. Tours her working loyalty. "No," she said, "and his clients are fine people who'd be an asset to your town, however temporary." She would have said more, except that at that moment the rod in her hand gave a strange little twist. "Oh," she mumbled, and then, "good Lord, my rod's starting to point."

"Jeehoshaphat!" Jed Alcott exclaimed. At his raised voice, a small crowd began to gather around them. "I can't believe how quickly you cottoned on to dowsing. Girl, you are a natural."

A hand dropped lightly onto her shoulder, shook it lightly, and she turned to see Ryan standing behind her. His eyes were full of approval. "I always knew you were a natural," he told her softly. "Good going."

Did he think she'd rigged this whole scene, faked the downpull of the dowsing rod? Indignantly she started to set him straight, but he'd gone over to stand next to Jed. She saw the satisfied glint in his eyes as Alcott introduced him to others among the spectators. Of course this had been his game plan all along.

Watching him, Cecily made herself a promise. No matter whether she worked for him or not, Ryan had to realize once and for all that she wasn't available to play games at his bidding.

5

"YOU'RE VERY QUIET," Ryan commented. "No fireworks, no calls for champagne? The victory of Whitwater is half yours by rights. You gave me the idea."

Behind her visor, Cecily frowned. Her hands tensed on the handlebars as Ryan's voice exuded confidence into the CB.

"You said the dowsers were in town, but once you told me Jed Alcott was a devotee, I made some inquiries and phoned Boston to get some research done on dowsing. The rest, as they say, is history."

So that was how he'd known all about Harding College. "I just wish you'd told me what you were going to do."

"Is that what's bothering you? I thought it was my formal presentation to the Whitwater selectmen that you didn't like."

She didn't even bother to answer that. His presentation that morning had been skillful, a blend of unassailable facts and the Alexander charm, and after yesterday's developments, there had been no contest. Cecily remembered how, after the dowsing demonstration, Jed Alcott had insisted on having Ryan meet his wife. This had led to an invitation for coffee, to which other "select" persons had been invited, and after that Ryan's game plan had gone smoothly.

There had been no hitches at the Monday meeting, either. The closest thing to opposition had come from a shrewd-eyed woman on the board who had pointed out that Ryan had a great number of irons in the fire. There was his Raya department-store chains and the subsidiary manufacturing plants he controlled to produce certain goods under the Raya trademark. With all this going on, how could a busy businessman like Ryan personally guarantee that the motorcycle tour coming through Whitwater would go without problems?

Jed Alcott had actually beamed approvingly when Ryan said he intended to conduct the tour himself. "Ryan A. Tours is successful because I personally make it so," he explained. Worldwide sales figures from his local plants proved his claim; so did letters from hotel owners and businesses and even from mayors, praising Ryan A. Tours' clientele and thanking him for his patronage. By the time he'd finished his presentation, the townsfolk were all in accord: Ryan's tour should be welcomed to Whitwater.

Surely he hadn't expected resistance? Cecily wasn't aware that she'd asked the question aloud until Ryan answered her over the CB.

"You make it sound like a military campaign. It was more complex than that. I wasn't dealing with backwater hicks, but with shrewd and farsighted business people. They gave me what I wanted because I offered them what they wanted." He paused. "I'm sorry I didn't tell you how I was going to approach Alcott, but you might have given the game away."

"'The game,'" she repeated, and suddenly Art and George came to mind. Had the thought of playing games ever occurred to them? Probably not. They were too busy making ends meet to worry about business strategy. A fan of sand and gravel from Ryan's wake pinged against her inner wheel, and she sighed. Some people were meant to make a lot of dust. The others sat by the roadside and ate it.

She said, "I want to say one thing. I didn't fake that dowsing-rod business."

"I was sure you didn't. You couldn't fake anything." She registered faint pleasure at the warmth in his voice, but then he spoiled the feeling by saying, "That's why I couldn't tell you ahead of time. A shrewd old-timer like Jed would have read you like a book."

She knew no way to say it except straight out. "I don't like game playing, Ryan."

"That's because you're not used to it." His voice was patient, reassuring. "I live in a very different world than Leeds Motorcycles, don't forget. The people I deal with all play by the same rules. You find an edge, an opportunity, and you take chances." She heard the frank relish in his voice before it changed. "And speaking of taking chances, Jed Alcott told me yesterday about a motorcycle route at the fork down the road. He said he rode it when he was a kid, and that the view was spectacular. Want to try it?"

Cecily glanced at the sun. The meeting with the selectmen had taken a long time, and sunset was coming fast. "You're the boss, but it's getting late.

How far do we have to ride to our next stop—Radley, isn't it?"

"Several hours, but we'd have to ride at night, anyway. Jed's route will only hold us up for half an hour or so. Are you game?"

She couldn't resist the challenge but when they turned left at the fork and left the winding country road for a narrow trail, she wasn't quite so sure she'd chosen wisely. The rutted, narrow trail began to climb almost immediately and then rose into a steep, almost-vertical slope. "According to Jed," Ryan explained as they avoided ruts in the road, "there's a fantastic view over the hill."

"It had better be fantastic. We should have dirt bikes for this kind of ground, and I'll bet there are bones of cyclists in the trees around here." When he laughed, she said, "Art used to tell me a ghoulish story about two cyclists trapped in the twilight zone—I'll bet he got the idea from a trail like this."

As she spoke they came over the top of the hill and into the blazing sunset. Cecily gasped, staring wide-eyed, at the huge red ball sinking between rock-faced mountains and inky-black pines. Sunlight painted the sweep of a valley below them with scarlet and orange gold. "Oh, wow," she said.

Ryan sounded as awed as she felt. "This view is worth that miserable ride, and I'm going to add it to the tour." He pointed toward the valley. "I believe that's Route 232 down there, so if we cut down this mountain we can get right onto it and hardly lose any time." He paused. "Problems, partner? You look thoughtful."

"No problems, no. I was just thinking that Art would love this view. When I phoned him last night he asked for all the details of the trip."

"And you told him everything?" he murmured, but she refused to rise to the bait.

"I wouldn't be able to describe this. The colors, the sun—even the awful road. I wish he could have come with you, Ryan. He'd have been a wonderful companion."

"So are you." He really seemed to mean it, and before she could get her guard up, pleasure rushed through her. "Besides, you can share all this when you get back. That's half the fun, I'm told."

He started his engine again and led the way down the hillside. The thick golden light splashed brilliance across the trees that had already started to turn gold and red, spinning copper lights over the back of Ryan's black helmet and his smooth riding leathers. In this light he looked to be a conqueror, an image somehow at variance with the quiet understanding of his last words to her. He was right—the telling of adventures made them even more precious. Art had enjoyed recounting his experiences every bit as eagerly as she had listened to them. She couldn't wait to tell him and the Zolichicks about her experience with the dowsing rod. Knowing Art, he'd go cut a fork of wood and walk around Clinton with it until George asked if he was demented. She grinned at the thought, then wondered whom Ryan would tell.

She didn't have to wonder—she knew. Ryan's audience wouldn't be a handful of family. No doubt, he'd tell stockbrokers and entrepreneurs, and of course there would be beautiful or influential women to entertain with his adventures in a small hick town. What would he say about his associate, about the naive woman hired on as a mechanic who was also a "natural" dowser?

Not liking the direction her thoughts had taken, Cecily kept her mind on the trail as it wound down the side of the mountain. Distances from the summit were deceptive; it was taking much longer to descend than they had first thought. When twilight came, they were still far from the valley and Route 232. The mountain air cooled rapidly. Though she was well protected by her leathers, Cecily felt the wind cutting against her cheeks, bringing with it the green smell of fir trees and grass and the moldy scent of fallen leaves.

"Are you still with me?" Ryan's voice over the CB broke the silence between them. "I don't think we have much farther to go. But perhaps it would be wiser for my clients to get back down the hill after watching the sunset."

"You could be right." As she spoke, she saw Ryan's motorcycle jolt. "Watch out!" she cried.

Before the words had even formed fully, the powerful bike in front of her went into skid, and as she shouted her warning, she saw the handlebars of Ryan's Electra Glide start to tip. She did the only thing she could, swinging clear to give him maneuvering room, but that wasn't good enough. Horrified, she saw Ryan go down, roll off and kick himself away from his machine. In the next moment, the Electra Glide and its rider had disappeared into the shadows by the side of the trail.

Panic tasted like bile in her throat as she called his name. There was no answer over the crackling CB, and she stopped her own motorcycle and dismounted hurriedly. Her fingers were clumsy with fear; her voice sounded scared even to her. "Ryan, are you all right? Ryan—answer me!"

Her only reply was the faint screech of a bat dipping low and brushing close to her. She disconnected her CB, turned her headlights toward the spot where Ryan and his cycle had gone down and then ran to the edge of the trail. "Ryan!" she called desperately.

"It's all right." The relief she felt at the sound of his voice made her light-headed, and now she saw a shadow detaching itself from the greater dark. "I managed to roll clear. I skidded on a patch of leaves on the road."

She hurried to him, scrunching through last year's dead leaves and prickly underbrush. He was on his feet when she got to him, and she caught him by the arms. Relief almost brought tears. "When I saw you go down I thought for sure you'd be trapped," she whispered. "Those were some great moves, mister."

He put an arm around her and gave her a quick hug. For a second her shaken body registered muscle and sinew, and then she felt him wince. "You're hurt. Where?"

He didn't reply.

"Your arm? Elbow? Thighs? Tell me, Ryan."

"Just bruises." He took his arm away from her and spoke almost abruptly. "Help me get the motorcycle up and out onto the trail. I'm more worried about what's happened to it."

He stalked off, and she followed, trying not to think of Art's stories about riders' legs being caught and crushed under their heavy machines. Thank

God, Ryan at least seemed unhurt. Yet when they found the Harley Electra Glide, she thought of weight again. They were going to have to right more than eight hundred pounds of metal before she could even check for damages.

In spite of the cold night air, she was sweating in her leathers as she helped Ryan attach the tow strap around the front fork of his machine, then round the rear seat and sissy bar of her Sportster. The next step took teamwork, and she was aware of Ryan's intense efforts as well as her own while she carefully rode her cycle away at an angle that slowly hauled the Electra Glide upright. This done, Ryan guided the cycle out of the woods and back on the trail.

"How bad is it?" he asked as Cecily knelt to run her hands and eyes over the motorcycle. She didn't answer him at once but frowned in concentration as she made her inventory. The lights had been smashed, and the fender over the front wheel had been badly bent. "Well?" Ryan demanded.

He had hunkered down beside her, and even at such a time she felt the impact of this closeness. When she breathed she realized that she drew in not woodland scents or the sour smell of earth, but the vital and clean fragrance of Ryan himself. "Not too bad—not that I can see, anyway. The front wheel's got to be taken off so that I can straighten out that fender, and I want to check the handlebars and the tires, of course."

He frowned. "How far can I ride it?"

"Not far at all. We could use the tow lines to take you to the nearest town, but I'll have to work on that fender before it digs into the front tire and ruins it."

He was silent for a moment. "We'll camp out, then. Just before I skidded and went down, I noticed a clearing near here. It's not the Whitwater Inn, but beggars can't be choosers."

If he felt pain, he showed nothing as he walked the Harley back up the trail until they found the clearing he'd seen. Here a glade of trees formed a natural wall on three sides. Once in the clearing, they could hear the ripple of running water. Cecily's headlight revealed that the clearing was covered with ferns and moss and spires of top-heavy goldenrod. "Not bad at all," she exclaimed, and at his nod she added, "Now I can check the Electra Glide—and I can see to you, too."

He had pushed his goggles up over his hair. She saw the dark eyebrows slant up. "Beg pardon, ma'am?" he drawled in wry imitation of a Hollywood cowboy.

"You heard me. I told you that Art's liniment was good for bruises and sprains, didn't I? There's no use fixing the cycle if you're too stiff to ride it tomorrow," she told him sternly. "You told me so yourself."

He didn't quite frown, but something in the way he held his big body told her he didn't care for the reminder. "Start on my machine, okay? I have a few things to do before swabbing myself with Art's concoction. I want to see how pure that water is, too. If we're lucky, it's a tributary of Mad Turkey River and clear as a bell."

Knowing there was no use arguing with him, Cecily turned her headlight directly on the damaged Electra Glide and began her repairs. She straightened the bent exhaust, checked the handlebars, gripped the front fender with one hand as she felt the steering-head bearing with the other. Ryan came back to her side while she was using sockets to remove the damaged front fender, and he helped to hammer out the dents.

"What else can be done?" he asked.

She ran her hands over the Electra Glide critically. "That's all for now. Tomorrow, as soon as we reach Radley, we'll find a reputable mechanic and a place where I can really get to work. The fender has to be properly repaired. The lights have to be replaced. And I'd like to give it a good going-over. You took a bad spill. It'll be some time before the motorcycle is roadworthy again."

"I'll take your word for it. Meanwhile, since we can't go anyplace tonight, we might as well enjoy the comforts of home."

She turned to look over her shoulder, and stared at the clearing. She had been so absorbed in her work that she hadn't realized what Ryan had been up to. He had ringed stones around a fire pit; a pan had been positioned over it. Enticing smells spilled out of the pan, while Ryan had spread his bedroll out to make a comfortable seat.

"You did all this while I was puttering around?" she exclaimed. "You're some kind of worker."

"We aim to please. Mind you, I can't vouch for the stew—it came out of a can. It's probably burned, too."

Burned or not, the food was good and hearty, and Cecily ate two helpings, mopping up the second with a slab of bread that emerged from Ryan's saddlebags. She said feelingly, "I'm glad you're here. I wouldn't have known the first thing about starting a fire in the open." She looked around her admiringly at his handiwork. "Did you father teach you about all this?"

He looked surprised, and she saw his eyes narrow slightly, as if against the smoke of the fire. "Hardly—he wasn't the outdoors type, and besides, he'd have been much too busy to play at camping out. I learned survival skills from an old Indian who used to work for my mother at her vacation home in Arizona." His voice deepened in remembrance. "Thomas took me out on overnights whenever mom was busy impressing houseguests. Once we spent a week high in the mountains. I remember watching the sun come up over those mountains and thinking that it was the most wonderful thing I'd ever seen."

He stopped talking, but Cecily had noted the bleakness in his voice. It reminded her of the expression she had seen in his eyes yesterday. Shadows. Shadows of what, she wondered. "Thomas seems like the ideal companion," she commented.

"Well, he tried. Tried to teach me to be a decent outdoors cook, too—but in that he wasn't so successful." Ryan put another stick on the fire, and his face was starkly outlined in flame, tension in the hard line of his cheek and jaw, tightness in his mouth. He didn't like to remember any of this, she realized. And yet he'd once told her good memories always helped.

Not liking the feel of the silence between them, she said lightly, "At least Thomas taught you about camping. The Leeds and the Zolichicks are all hopeless in the outdoors. Once George and Edna took me with them when they went hiking, and I was so incredibly dumb I picked poison ivy because I thought it was pretty. You'd better believe I was a mess the next day."

"But Art pasted you with his ointment," Ryan murmured.

He had leaned back, almost reclining on his spread-out bedroll, his face in shadow, so that she couldn't tell whether he was laughing or not. "Yes, he did. And don't get too comfortable, because you know what I'm going to say next—it's your turn for treatment."

"It probably smells like skunk oil," he groaned, but he remained still as she got up and rummaged in her saddlebags.

"First let me see your arms," she said when she came back with the jar.

She saw a curious reluctance in his gray eyes. "This isn't necessary. I was hardly scratched."

"Liar."

Moving slowly, Ryan unzipped his leather jacket and peeled off his cotton shirt. As it slipped off, firelight bronzed the skin of his chest and turned the dark mat of chest hair to shadow, but for now she had eyes only for his hurts. His entire right shoulder and arm were a mass of bruises. Discolored, already purpling, they curled from shoulder to elbow. "Good Lord," she said, "and you hauled up that bike by yourself."

He began to rub the ointment into his skin. "I had very competent help."

You're not doing it right," she protested, and taking the jar from him, covered her hands with the stuff and kneaded it into the muscle itself. "This way, you won't have a stiff arm. I'm sorry if I'm hurting you, but believe me, you'll be grateful in the morning."

Ryan was oddly silent under her touch, and the hard arm and shoulder seemed even harder now with tension. His demeanor bothered her, cut through her concern for him and made her suddenly conscious of what she was doing. She hadn't been aware until now of the way the campfire leaped over the hard power of his body. Her heart started to hammer as she rubbed the ointment over his collarbone and touched, with the heel of her hand, a thick curl of his chest fur. How would it feel to be pressed against his bare chest? Hastily she pushed away that thought.

"Are you finished?" His voice was abrupt, and shattered through her thoughts, making her start. "I'm not used to being fussed over."

His tone surprised her. "Don't be foolish. On the road you have to work as a team. Now you know the ointment works, so if you have any other painful spots, you go ahead and use it."

He took the ointment from her and held the jar in his hand. For a moment he looked at it, and then back to her. His expression was contrite, his smile rueful and oddly appealing. "I'm sorry," he said. "That was rude of me, Cecily. The thing is that I'm not used to people doing things for me, on the road or anywhere else."

"You like to rely on yourself."

He nodded. "Old habits are hard to break. But you're right. If I didn't know it before, I've learned that much tonight. I couldn't have managed without you."

"Just your average teamwork." She wanted to keep it light, but all at once that was difficult. Her awareness of him had deepened, intensified. As he leaned closer to the heat and positioned another piece of wood, firelight softened the strong planes of his face and made him seem younger. She thought of Ryan as a boy kneeling at the edge of another campfire somewhere in Arizona, listening eagerly to kindly Thomas. That younger Ryan had yearned for the warmth and companionship of his parents, and found nothing. No wonder he'd told her she and Art were lucky to have each other....

"Don't." She heard the new note in his deep voice and realized he'd read her thoughts. Troubled, she turned to him, and when she saw the traces of an old loneliness in his eyes, she didn't stop to think. She reached out to him, took his hands in hers.

There was a moment when all the world seemed to stop. Everything was so quiet Cecily could hear the gurgle of the water nearby, the sigh of the wind in the treetops, could hear her heart beating a wild alarm. She started to pull her hands back but it was too late. Ryan tugged them gently, and then she was in his arms.

She had never been kissed like this. His mouth rubbed against hers, relearning the boundaries of pleasure before he took her lower lip between his teeth, nibbling delicately. Her lips parted under his insistence, and he touched them with his tongue, caressing them. Boldly he penetrated the satin secrets of her inner mouth.

Her eyelids fluttered over her eyes, but not before she'd seen herself reflected in his fire-warmed eyes. Then, as his mouth possessed hers, she felt him tug at the zipper of her leather jacket, her back cooled by the wind as the leather dropped to the ground and he began to unfasten the buttons on her shirt. She murmured something—protest or agreement, she didn't know which—and responding, he lifted her across his knees. He held her cradled against his hard chest and hard thighs while he pulled impatiently at her shirt bottom, releasing it from her leather pants. Under the fabric, his fingertips stroked and courted her bare skin, and she shivered with pleasure as his questing thumb rubbed lightly over her still-covered nipples.

Against the lace of her bra, her teased breasts yearned for his touch, until that barrier and her shirt, too, slid away from her. Only then did his mouth leave hers to seek other pleasure.

It was dark; it was cold, but Cecily wasn't chilled. Her senses were singing with yearning for Ryan and she clasped him close to exult in the rough tenderness of his stubbled cheek against the inner curve of her breasts, the passion of his open-mouthed kisses. Drugged pleasure imploded as he teased, nudging her coral areolas and then her taut nipples with his tongue.

"Please," she whispered, and heard him laugh deep in his throat, a wholly male sound of satisfaction and desire.

"Please what, sweetheart? Does this please you?"

Ripples of delight undulated through her as he took the ready buds of her breasts into his mouth, teasing, sucking while his hands wandered over the curves of her hips and legs. Easily he snapped open her riding slacks, and she lifted her hips to help him as he slid the leather from her eager flesh. Sensitive fingers smoothed over her thighs and between them, and at his touch, she began to move to a primal rhythm.

His lips left her breasts to take her mouth again, his tongue thrusting, aping another passionate invasion. He continued to cradle her to him so that his chest rubbed her tender nipples, a contact that made her ache for more. Then, as if possessing a life of their own, her fingers tugged at the buckle of his belt, at the metal rasp of zipper, until below the sheath of clothes she touched the hardness of his want for her.

"I need to love you." Ryan's voice was husky between passionate kisses, and she murmured her soft assent against his mouth. Desiring him made her tremble as his suddenly tense arms lowered her gently onto his bedroll, and she shivered erotically at the contrast between the smooth, cool cotton at her back and the warm, furred male chest pressed at her breasts. His hands and mouth seemed to touch her everywhere, on her mouth, her breasts, her belly and thighs. When he caught the sides of her lace bikini panties and tugged, she raised her hips to help him.

In a moment she would be completely naked. As would he. She wanted that, wanted him so much that at first she thought the beating noise nearby was the drumming of her own pulse. It was only when it came again that she realized something was rustling in the underbrush near them. Ryan had heard it, too. She could feel him grow tense and watchful against her for a moment, and then relax.

"Hush, sweetheart, it's nothing. Just some animal in the bushes." His arms tightened around her as he promised, "I'll keep you safe from birds that go bump in the night."

His words echoed in the muzziness of her mind. He had called her "sweetheart," said he'd keep her safe. A part of her wanted to believe him, to return to the warm safety of his hard embrace and his mind-dizzying kisses. It was too late; warning bells were already screaming in her brain.

Cecily put the palms of her hands against his broad chest and gave it a little push. "No," she tried to say, but her mouth felt rubbery, and her throat didn't produce sound. She shook her head, instead. *Please, no more.*

Ryan understood her unspoken plea, and for a moment she saw his eyes narrow, saw the raw passion that had been kindled between them struggle with control. Did she even want to stop him? Before she could decide, the look in his eyes changed, and the tension eased from his body.

She found her voice. "This isn't what either of us are here for, Ryan." She managed a shaky laugh. "I guess we were both carried away by the ambience—mysterious woods, roaring campfire, the great outdoors...."

"You didn't mention my fabulous cooking, but I forgive you." To her relief, he matched her attempt at lightness. For a moment longer he held her. Then he let her go. Abruptly, she was aware of night air goose-pimpling her bare back and arms and thighs, of her near nakedness. She drew her arms across her breasts as he kissed the top of her head and swung to his feet in a movement both graceful and totally without embarrassment. There was nothing hurried in the way he fastened his trousers, pulled up his leather jacket. Then he said, "Talking about mysterious woods and the great outdoors, perhaps I'd better check to see if there's really something crawling around in those bushes."

He could have been announcing that he was taking a stroll before turning in, but as he moved away from the fire and her, Cecily realized she still couldn't breathe very easily. She wished she could think clearly. Yet only one thought formed in the jumble of her mind: no doubt Ryan was used to mixing pleasure with business. Maybe he even expected as much. But she wasn't about to let this happen again.

She didn't dare.

6

CECILY WAS UNPACKING her saddlebags when Ryan returned to the glade. Outwardly calm, she still needed the solid, metallic presence of the motorcycles to reassure her and redefine her reason for being here with him.

He seemed to have no such problem; his reassuring nod to her was cheerful. "All secure," he said. "No enemies at the gates, no monsters lurking in the bushes. We can both relax."

She knew better. Even though she'd had time to get her thoughts and priorities straightened out, his deep voice did something to her pulse. She took a deep, bracing breath and said, "Ryan, we need to talk."

"Come back where it's warm." He had hunkered down by the fire, a lean figure etched in jet against the orange glow. She hesitated. "Suit yourself," he said, "but you have to be freezing back there. One thing about New England, the nights turn cold early."

It hadn't felt cold in his arms—Hastily she dismissed the treacherous thought and searched for the right words. "In Boston we agreed that I was to come along with you and give you advice on the trip and make sure the motorcycles were properly maintained. I think it's time we went back to the letter of that contract."

She didn't know which annoyed her more, the way her emotional balance swayed when those sea-gray eyes swung toward her, or the amusement that glinted in them. "Lighten up, Cecily. We're of age, and sex is legal."

She knew she couldn't show weakness now. "I'm sure that's true, but I didn't come with you for sex," she told him sturdily. "I came to do a job."

Cecily had thought he might argue or try in some other way to reestablish their earlier closeness, but to her surprise, he nodded. "Teamwork, you said." He nudged a slow-burning log with the toe of his boot as he added thoughtfully, "We both worked hard out on the trail tonight, partner. Danger and work bring people closer."

He was right, of course. Art had often said as much about the camaraderie that resulted from shared adventure, and their embrace had no doubt been a reaction to the hazards on the trail. The thought brought relief and an odd twinge of disappointment she didn't want to analyze. "You could be right," she said, "but I still want your word on this, Ryan. No more of these..."

"Romantic interludes?" He got to his feet in the swift, easy way she had noted earlier, coming to stand a few feet from her. Involuntarily she took a step back, and he raised both hands in an exaggerated gesture of surrender. "Don't worry, fair maiden, your virtue is safe with me. The trouble is that you're so damned desirable. Did you know that the firelight turns your hair to red-gold flame?" He grinned suddenly. "If you looked like George, for instance, there'd be no problem."

"I think we've said everything that needs to be said," she muttered. "I don't know about you, but it's been a long day, and I'm getting some sleep now. I want to get your motorcycle to Radley as soon as possible in the morning."

He helped her spread a tarp over the motorcycles; then while she unpacked her bedroll and blankets, he walked back to the fire to bank the flames for the night. "You'd best bed down near the fire," he told her. "It's going to turn colder, and you'll need the warmth."

She tried to ignore him as she arranged her bed for the night, but her attention kept shifting. The sound of him unzipping his leather jacket grated loudly in the dark silence, and she was very aware of him pulling off his boots and removing his shirt and belt. Unzipping his leather pants, he spoke in a matter-of-fact voice. "Best way to sleep in cold weather is in the buff. Your bedroll traps your body heat and keeps you warmer."

Involuntarily her eyes swung toward him as he peeled off his leathers. For a moment firelight played over his broad, bare chest, lean waist, hard-muscled thighs and tight dark briefs. She turned hastily away as he said helpfully, "Don't knock it till you've tried it. Things are different out on the trail, Cecily."

For once she agreed with him wholeheartedly, and removed her jacket and boots before sliding into her sleeping bag. Only then did she unzip and remove her leather slacks. As she was folding them to form a pillow, her finger connected with something hard that had been pushed into the folds of her bedroll.

She pulled out the small notepad with a pen clipped to it.

So much had happened since they had left Boston that for a moment its presence in her sleeping bag baffled her. Then she remembered what she'd told Leonard Coxe from *Intro* about taking notes for a possible article. She started to put pen and pad away, but hesitated. She had wanted to jot down some notes so that she could remember details of their adventures to tell Art and the Zolichicks, and besides, writing had always been therapeutic for her. A long time ago, when she was still healing from the shock of her mother's death, writing down her thoughts had eased the pain in her heart. Perhaps writing down her resolutions about her relationship with Ryan would put things into perspective now.

"Sweet dreams." The deep voice broke into her thoughts, and Cecily turned swiftly to look at him. He was propped up on one elbow, his bare torso gleaming bronze in the flames, and the warmth of his smile was tantalizing. She frowned as she turned away to pick up her pen. Definitely, she thought, it was time to get some perspective.

THE NEXT DAY they stopped in Radley for repairs, after which they crossed through Vermont into New York. Veering away from cities, they rode the back routes, some of which had sharp curves that limited speeds to fifteen miles per hour. Used to thinking of skyscrapers in connection with the state, Cecily enjoyed the rich woodlands and clear creeks and covered bridges they passed on their first day in New York State.

She and Ryan had intended to stop at an inn where, he said, both Ben Franklin and Thomas Jefferson had stayed. But they were so far behind schedule because of the damage done to Ryan's motorcycle that they had to forgo this. The delay cost them in other ways, as well. What had been planned as a leisurely crossing of New York State became a swift perusal of the proposed tour route and available inns.

Even so, Cecily discovered points of interest not on the proposed route. Their two-day trip through the state led them past the town of Jennings, where, Ryan explained, Raya department store had its subsidiary manufacturing plants. Though they didn't stop, the fact that those plants existed was another reminder of Ryan's wealth and influence, and she jotted Jennings down in her journal.

She didn't have much time to write about anything else until they'd crossed into New Jersey. Once there, their pace became more leisurely. Leaving the main highway, they made their way toward the Delaware Water Gap and stopped just short of it near Colesville, at the elegant Sanders Inn. Cecily admitted that it was a far cry from the nondescript motel they had stayed in the night before.

She found the inn's ambience welcome and refreshing, but though he agreed, Ryan was at his most critical. "This is the only luxury my clients will get before Trenton. After this, they'll have the Kittatiny Mountains and the Pine Barrens to cope with, so this place has got to be first-class. I want your feedback on the accommodations, the service and the food."

They tested the last two in a secluded corner of an unabashedly romantic dining room, and found the service prompt, courteous and without flaw. The food was delicious. After a relaxing dinner, Cecily carried a glass of Nebbiolo up to her room and settled down for a long chat with Art.

He listened to her various adventures and then chuckled with pleasure. "Aha. So you and Ryan have started working together. Takes a couple days, I know, but once you get the rhythm, everything clicks." He paused. "I'll bet Ryan carries his weight on the trip, too."

"Yes, he does." Cecily stared down into the clear heart of her wine and frowned at it. She had to admit that rich man or not, Ryan was a hard worker who quickly learned all she taught him about maintenance and repair. His sense of humor made him a good companion on the road—a perfect companion, really—except that she wasn't quite at ease with him. Their relationship had been professional since the night of his accident, and yet...

"You like him. I thought you would," Art was saying. "Liked him myself, right off, and so did George. Ryan's quite a man."

Her father's innocent words conjured up an image of Ryan near a campfire, his bare, muscled chest etched against darkness, bronzed by flame. Hastily, before the image could conjure up others, Cecily changed the subject. "How's business?"

Art was delighted to talk shop. "I've never been busier, Ceci. We've been getting calls from lots of people who want to buy motorcycles from us or get their bikes fixed." She could see his grin as vividly as if he were standing before her. "Even George is purring like a kitten."

She wanted to speak to George, too, but he and Edna were out when she called. Instead the Zolichicks telephoned her early the next morning, just as she was packing, and after Edna had asked motherly questions about her health and warned her to eat and sleep well and dress warmly, George got on the phone. "Got your hotel's name from Art," he rumbled. "Edna and me wanted to hear your voice."

Something in his tone made her frown. "Is something wrong?" When he hesitated a second, she was sure. "Come on, George, give. Is the shop in trouble?"

George growled, "Not the shop—it's as happy as a dog with fleas. It's his goddamned arthritis, Cecily. He's been waking up all cramped and sore, and working alone isn't helping much. You know how stubborn the man is. He won't hire an assistant, insists he can't afford one yet. Matt came back on the weekend to help, but he's got to go to school, too."

She bit her lip. She could imagine Art working too hard, determined to make a success of Leeds Motorcycles in spite of the pain and stiffness in his joints. "Should I come home?" she asked uncertainly.

"Don't talk foolishness." George sounded horrified. "If Art knew I'd told you about his aches and pains, he'd never let me hear the end of it. I shouldn't have mentioned it and worried you, except that maybe next time you talk to that stubborn mule-brained old goat, you might try and convince him to hire some help until you come home."

Home, Cecily thought. A part of her yearned for the dusty garage while another part—equally insistently—whispered of trails that led into golden sunsets and through a mysterious wilderness of pines.

As she said goodbye, she couldn't hold back a small sigh.

"Trouble?" She was surprised to see Ryan standing in the doorway. He was packed and ready, his helmet under his arm. "I didn't mean to eavesdrop, but your door was open, and you sounded upset. Is something wrong in Clinton?"

"George growls a lot, but he cares for Art. He told me Art's arthritis is bad again."

"Rough on a man like that," was all he said, but she read understanding in his voice, and when she met his eyes she saw in them a concern that said more than any words. "If you want to call and talk to him, go ahead. Take all the time you need. I'll meet you outside when you're ready."

The genuine caring in his voice brought a lump to her throat. "Thank you, but it's not necessary. Art wouldn't like it if I worried about him. Anyway, it's not your problem [illegible] it's mine."

"Anything that matters to you is important to me." His words brought warmth that seemed to flow toward her, surround her, take away the sting of her wor[illegible]. Then she realized that she'd misread him, that his main concern was for the trip. And rightly so, she told herself. After all, she was a professional here to do a job. What was or wasn't happening at home had nothing to do with what she was being paid for.

Determinedly she put her private worries aside. As they left the quiet elegance of their hotel and rode toward the Delaware Water Gap, she concentrated on going over the day's scheduled travel route with Ryan. When they reached Old Mile Road, they were still discussing the possibility of veering off the main highway and following some scenic country road that would take them to Trenton. The beauty of the scenery took all words away, and they rode in awed silence.

Below them the Delaware River shimmered like silver, and sunlight lay gentle against early fall colors that mingled with the green of the Kittatiny Mountains. Each new vista was more magnificent than the last, and Cecily could hardly tear her eyes away to watch where she was going. They followed the Old Mile Road to various vantage points, then stopped at a spot overlooking a foaming gorge. Across the spumes of milk-white water they could see, parallel to the river, the Appalachian Trail running northward.

There really were no words expansive enough to contain all this beauty, but Cecily couldn't bear not to try. "I've never seen anything so grand and terrible and lovely," she said, sighing.

He turned to look at her quizzically. "You sound a bit sad."

"Do I? I didn't mean to." His eyes continued to hold hers, and she said, "I suppose I was thinking about Art again. He and I used to talk about going on the Appalachian Trail. It was one of those daydreams we put together over the atlas in our living room."

"But you never did hike the tail. Why not?"

"We couldn't afford it," she replied frankly. "I was at school for a while, and then Leeds Motorcycles had hard times, and after that Art's health started to slip."

"The arthritis." His deep voice was soft, hardly audible over the roar of the water below. "I don't blame you for missing him the way you do. Art's the kind of man anyone would want for a father."

Instead of the one he had.... The thought came so swiftly that for a horrible moment Cecily was afraid she'd spoken the words. Hastily she said, "Well, never mind. Art and I can still come here. When I tell him about all this gorgeous scenery, wild horses won't keep him away."

"Of course," he said, but she saw the look in his eyes alter subtly, and she realized again how different her world was from Ryan's. She couldn't imagine that he'd ever been denied anything. "The envy of every man and every woman's fantasy...." Leonard Coxe's words brushed once more against her mind and then vanished as she glanced at Ryan. In profile, his fine, strong face was thoughtful. When he turned to her, she saw a flicker of sadness in his eyes.

It was gone at once, and he was smiling when he said, "This place is going to be magnificent in the spring. I couldn't have asked for a more dramatic side trip for my clients. The river will be powerful with thaw. Maybe Art will come with us that time."

She stared at him. "You know I won't be coming with you in the spring."

"Slip of the tongue," he said, but there was a glint in his eyes. "Anyway, perhaps you'll enjoy yourself so much this trip that you'll come back. I have several satisfied customers who keep signing on for more of my tours."

"Ah, but you forget I'm not a customer," she retored, and turning away from the view, walked over to her cycle to pull out a roadmap. "From here we take 94 to Lafayette and then pick up 206," she said briskly. "We've got at least a hundred miles to go today. If you want to keep off the major highways and explore back roads that will take us into Trenton, we'd better be going."

"So we should." Sand and gravel crunched underfoot as he, too, left the view and walked toward his motorcycle. There he stopped and turned to her. "No, I hadn't forgotten. I'm glad you're no client on this trip." He seemed to hesitate before saying, "I couldn't ask for a better partner."

Looking up at him, she wasn't sure whether it was the sun reflected in his eyes that dazzled her. She tried to think of some suitable reply and couldn't frame the words. A cool breeze ruffled his dark hair, then brushed her cheek like a caress. Like his caress. In spite of all the barriers she had erected against a moment like this, she felt part of her deepest self reach out to him.

"I think you're giving me too much credit," she managed to say.

"Credit where credit is due, ma'am." He took her hand and dropped a light kiss on the palm. Automatically, she tried to pull her hand away, but his firm, strong clasp held it prisoner, and he lifted it for a moment to his cheek. Under the just-kissed sensitivity of her palm, she felt the hard line of his jaw, the rough-smooth coolness of his cheek. "I doubt if I'd have come this far without your know-how and hard work."

Cecily felt a muscle in his hard cheek leap against her palm a moment. Then he let go of her hand and walked toward the Electra Glide, pulling on his helmet and visor as he went. Disturbed as always by the strength of her reaction to him, she tried to match his ease of tone. "I don't believe that for a moment. Wherever we go people are eager to do anything for you."

He shrugged. "That's because they want something from me." He started his engine, and the roar drowned out his voice for a moment. Over the CB, he added, "People always have an angle. I've learned that if I offer them what they want—glamour, perhaps, or profit or excitement—they respond the way I want them to."

"Games," she murmured.

"Call them 'business strategies,' if you want. Some, of course, are more ruthless than others. The great Desmond Alexander's personal creed was, 'Use them before they have a chance to use you.' Not very noble, but it obviously worked for him."

She hadn't heard him speak so bluntly before; the stark words contrasted harshly to the way he'd spoken of Art earlier. She thought about that for a moment as they veered off Old Mile Road onto a country road they had hoped might be a good tour prospect. Hope soon faded. Though the route was scenic, it was also in such poor condition that all their concentration was needed to avoid potholes and ruts.

By afternoon they had decided to abandon it, and they stopped to discuss strategy over lunch at at small roadside restaurant. The restaurant owner suggested Harnessway Road. "You can't miss it," he told them enthusiastically. "I used to own a cycle when I was a kid, and I'd scoot down that old Harnessway Road as if I owned it. There's no traffic to speak of, just nice, rolling hills and great scenery.

You can pick up the main highway near Allerton after the Pohatcong Mountains."

Ryan looked at Cecily. "What do you say, partner?"

They consulted their map, and Cecily said, "Let's go for it. I like the idea of following new roads, and if we can connect with 206, there's no problem about reaching Trenton tonight. Besides, that's why you brought me along—to see whether certain roads would be too hard on motorcycles."

He grinned, "So you keep reminding me."

For the first two hours, the country road was as advertised. The sometimes-narrow, often-tricky route led up the rolling Pohatcong Mountains. Cecily knew Ryan's clients were good riders, and they would feel the same exhilaration that filled her as she sighted the silver curve of a river below them, the sharp rise of hills above. In fact, the way was so scenic and challenging that when they reached Allerton, they decided to stay on it awhile longer before swinging onto the main highway.

The detour was a mistake. Fifteen miles out of town, the route they were on turned rocky, sandy. Riding was hard. Cecily suggested turning back to Allerton, while Ryan was for pushing on. "According to the map, we can pick up 206 at Lansing, just over these hills," he explained. "If we go slowly, there'll be no trouble."

"You're the boss." Then frowned. "Oh-oh."

"Trouble?" His voice was crisp on the word.

"I'm afraid so. My lights just dimmed. The alternator's gone. If we don't get to Lansing soon, we'll be in really hot water, Ryan."

7

HE SWORE SOFTLY. "Your battery should keep you going for a good thirty miles or so, shouldn't it? We'll be in Lansing by then."

She looked around her at the country they were traveling through. In the dusk it appeared deserted, desolate. The silhouettes of lonely trees seemed to dip down the mountainside as far as she could see. "Shouldn't we turn back?" she asked worriedly.

"We must be halfway between Allerton and Lansing by now, and I think Lansing is the bigger town. You'd have a better chance of finding a repair shop that carries alternators for Harley Sportsters."

In the next half-hour, Cecily remembered the old song her mother had sung to her when she was a child, about the bear that went over the mountain. She almost hummed it loudly when they crested their third hill and saw yet another valley dipping in front of them, with no sign of town lights. "I should have known better than to trust a country mile," Ryan said. "How are you holding up back there?"

"Not too well. My lights keep getting dimmer."

"Hang tight, partner, and I'll get you to Lansing." His reply was cheerful, reminding her that unlike her, Ryan had faced situations far more difficult than a failing alternator on a mountain road. He was saying, "Think of how you'll be able to scare the daylights out of George and Art when you tell them about this. Better still, write it all down in your travelogue before you go to bed tonight. Then you can read the more harrowing passages to them."

So he knew she was keeping a journal—trust Ryan not to miss anything. No doubt he thought it some kind of travel diary. He wasn't far wrong, although the thought of some of the soul-searching she'd also done by way of that notebook wasn't too comfortable. "Didn't you ever keep a journal when you went mountain climbing or hang gliding?" she asked.

"No time, and besides, looking back at things isn't my sytle. I'd rather look forward—for instance to a good steak and a cold beer in Lansing." Just then, they crested a hill. "There it is."

Below them in the distance were twinkling lights against the deep-indigo sky. "Thank the Lord," she said with a groan.

"I told you I'd get you here." As they started down the hill Ryan added, "Ease up. We're coming to a sharp turn."

The powerful sweep of his headlights caught the turn; her own lights barely flickered. *Come on,* she begged her battery silently, *hold up a little longer.* Then, as she went into the curve, she knew it wouldn't. "The battery's going, Ryan," she called into the CB. "I'm going to come out of this turn and then stop."

"Can you handle it?"

She said she could, but as she applied the brakes, the battery died. One moment she was riding a responsive, powerful machine; the next she was straddling dead weight. As the engine shut down she could hear the wind, and then her immediate surroundings turned black. In darkness she tried to steer the suddenly stiff and awkward Sportster toward the side of the road. A spray of sand and dirt pinged against the insides of her small fenders, against her legs and gloved hands. Then, mercifully, the motorcycle went quiet under her.

Cecily pulled her helmet off and let the night wind blow through her hair. As she dismounted from her useless Sportster, she saw Ryan circling back toward her. In the next moment he had pulled up, cut his own engine and was coming toward her. "All right?"

His voice was sharp with concern, so that she answered hastily, "I'm fine—but it's still a long way to town." The cold wind wrapped its fingers through her hair, and she shivered. "You'll have to tow me." She looked doubtfully down the steep mountain road. "It won't be easy."

"No, but we'll manage." His calmness was steadying, as was the arm he put around her shoulders. For once there was nothing sensual in the embrace. She leaned gratefully into its strength and support as he added, "I've never towed another cycle, so you'll have to tell me what to do."

"You just have to ride slowly, and I have to make sure the towline stays taut between us." He nodded. "Attaching the line to the bikes is no problem."

Cecily knew she should get the line at once, but she remained where she was. The tension of riding her fading cycle over the mountains was ebbing away in the circle of his arms, and she was reluctant to move. Warmth and comfort seemed to flow from his big body to hers, but as she hesitated, another awareness stirred deep within her blood. A different tension trembled through her.

Ryan's strong arms no longer offered friendly safety. Like a night-blooming flower, her body was opening, yearning toward his nearness. Her breasts felt heavy, waiting; her loins had been warmed with familiar honey. Taut and ready, her nipples strained against the lace of her bra, and as she shifted, the rub of soft lace against the distended buds recalled another touch. She tried to summon reason, to brace herself again this invasion of all her senses....

"Are you sure?" His voice was husky suddenly in the dark, and she felt the brush of his thumb against her cheek, tracing the line of her jaw, her lower lip. At his touch the blood in her veins seemed to sizzle as if water droplets had been scorched by flame. She felt dazed, giddy, totally off balance. She wasn't sure of anything.

"Sure." She heard herself repeat the word in the smallest of whispers.

"After all, I don't want to lose you on the mountain road." His voice was still husky, and he cleared his throat. She realized then that he was talking about towing her. A wave of emotion that was part relief and part loss eddied through the confusion of her senses.

"It's simple, really." She was grateful she sounded so positive. "Let me get the line, and I'll show you."

Moving with careful and self-conscious deliberation, acting as if the moment in his arms hadn't been important to her, she stepped away from the curve of his arm. Immediately she felt the raking of the wind, cold around her. It penetrated even the warmth of her leather jacket, and she shivered as she pulled out the towline. "You hook the line around your carrying frame. I pass the other side around the frame of my cycle, under the lights." She demonstrated, then explained how it was possible to keep the line taut between them.

As always he was a quick learner, and as they rode slowly down the mountain road toward the lights of the town, she wondered at his skill and concentration. Perhaps that was Ryan's secret—that he undertook each thing he did with the same single-minded will to succeed. For a moment she focused again on her notebook in her saddlebag recalling Leonard Coxe's words about the public paying almost anything to learn about Ryan Alexander's secret heart.

At this point, she wasn't sure she even wanted to know the private man. Indifference wasn't what she felt, either. It was more like self-preservation.

THEY RODE INTO LANSING an hour later. It was an hour fraught with tension and the difficulty of maintaining an even pace around mountain turns that could often be tricky or downright dangerous, and Cecily breathed a frank sigh of relief when her Harley Sportster coasted into the town. Her relief was short-lived. It seemed as though the small town had done everything but roll up its streets at dusk, and Ryan's headlights glinted off shuttered windows.

The Big K Garage, the first garage they found, was as tightly shut as the other stores. They later dicovered it was the only garage in Lansing, located at the Pastoral Motel, a smallish but respectable establishment on the edge of town.

Patty Baker, the motel's amiable owner, gave them the information. "Everybody knows everybody's business in a small town," she told them shrewdly. "You need a mechanic, so you need Ezra Kinkaid. This being Friday, Ezra should be having his steak at the Palace. Steak's on special tonight, with salad, rolls and fries for $5.95. Want me to get him on the phone? He's an old curmudgeon, but he does good work."

A phone call rousted out the owner of the Big K. He agreed to meet them in an hour's time. He sounded gruff over the phone, and their first glimpse of him confirmed Pat Baker's assessment of his character. Ezra was tall, slope jawed, with graying hair and shrewd blue eyes. He hadn't heard anything about Alexander Industries or Ryan A. Tours, but he thawed marginally when he learned Cecily was Arthur Leeds's daughter. "Saw your dad once out at Daytona," he growled. "That was one whopper of a race. He won it, too, as I recall." He paused briefly, "Now about the alternator. I don't carry one that'll fit a '68 Sportster, so I'll have one ordered from Trenton."

"To save time I could have it driven out here," Ryan suggested, but Ezra's jaw hardened stubbornly.

"I do business with only one supplier in Trenton, and that's who I aim to contact about the alternator. Tomorrow being Saturday, I doubt he can find one for me before Monday, but I'll give it a try." He folded his arms and all but glared at Ryan. "If you don't like it," his expression said, "lump it."

Laughter bubbled to Cecily's lips as she saw several emotions chase one another across Ryan's mobile face. Finally he shrugged. "All right, order the alternator. How long will it take?"

"Depending. The weekend's coming up. Maybe two, maybe three days," Ezra Kinkaid rumbled.

"Three days!" Ryan exploded.

The garage owner leveled a finger at him. "Trouble with you young city fellows, you don't take life easy. You're in some mighty pretty country, so what's wrong with enjoying it? Go out to one of the state parks. They're mighty pretty this time of year. Or ride down to them pine barrens. You won't feel so rushed when you're exploring that part of the state."

Before Ryan could reply, Cecily tactfully intervened and asked if she could help install the alternator when it came in. Ezra said he thought that might be all right. "Guess Arthur Leeds trained his daughter to be a good wrench," he said grudgingly. He added for Ryan's benefit, "But I don't hold with any kind of interference from folks who don't know a wrench from their elbow."

Afraid that Ryan might have reached the boiling point, Cecily thanked the mechanic and practically dragged her employer out of the shop. As they walked to Ryan's motorcycle, she glanced up at him. "I had the feeling that if you said anything more he'd go even slower," she explained.

To her surprise, he laughed. "Can't say I blame the old cuss. Here comes some young city slicker waving money in his face and telling him his business. In a way, it's a good thing this happened. I hadn't thought of it, but now I'll make certain there are spare parts compatible with my clients' motorcycles available along the tour route."

Trust Ryan to capitalize on something that to a lesser man might have been disaster. "You're right, of course," she said. "I should have thought of that."

"That's why we're doing this dry run. And as the old gent said, we can go and visit the pine barrens. We'd intended to, anyway, and we might as well do something while your bike is in the shop."

She demurred. "I doubt if I can rent a cycle hereabouts."

"We can ride tandem." He swung a leg over his Electra Glide. "How else did you expect to get back to the Pastoral Motel?"

Wordlessly she snapped on her helmet and visor and took her place behind him. As she did so, she was racked by a sense of déjà vu. Carefully she positioned herself, and he said, "Hang on. As I pointed out on the mountain, I don't want to lose you."

Even though she had cautioned herself against reacting to his closeness, nevertheless she was unprepared as she circled his hard torso with her arms. His whipcord-lean body was still steel and silk under her arms, and she felt tension in his stomach muscles as the powerful motorcycle surged forward. Momentum pressed her forward against him. With the impact of softness again hardness, memories overwhelmed her as devastating as fiery kisses.

"What do you think of the pine-barrens idea?" he was asking her, and she forced herself to concentrate on the here and now. "It's about sixty or seventy miles as the crow flies, so we should be able to make a good day's trip out of it."

Her laughter was shaky. "More country roads?"

As she spoke he pulled into the Pastoral Motel's parking lot and cut the engine and lights. In the sudden darkness she could hear autumn insects chirping loudly, the sound of his even breathing as he turned to face her. "Have you had enough excitment for a while?" There was real concern in his voice. "We've kept up a pretty stiff pace, and I'd forgotten you're not used to this. Why not rest up tomorrow? If I know Mr. Ezra Kinkaid, it'll take him four days, not three, to get your motorcycle fixed."

She got off the cycle and looked at him uncertainly. "But your schedule..."

"Don't worry about that." He, too, dismounted, pulling off helmet and gloves as he spoke. "You're my partner on this trip. I was wrong this evening in not going back to Allerton, so you call the shots for tomorrow."

He was sincere. In the dim light of the motel office, she saw that he was smiling—not the practiced, charming smile she was so familiar with, but one that could almost be called tender. It confused her.

"If we do go to the pine barrens, how long would it take?"

"Two hours down, two hours back, and we'd have the rest of the day to sightsee. It's supposed to turn warm tomorrow—Indian summer, Pat Baker said."

A beautiful day and Ryan... Inexplicably her heart tugged with happiness. She couldn't name or give a reason for that surge of joy, but it helped make up her mind. "Let's try the pine barrens. As Ezra said, we should take time to enjoy."

"You're not only a good wrench, Ms Leeds, you're a good sport." Something in his many-shaded voice alerted her to the fact that though they were discussing business, something was stirring on a deeper level. But then he continued casually, "Better let me walk you to your room. Lansing looks like a nice little place, but you can't be too careful with small towns. Once I stopped at a quaint town in the southwest and found a rattler in my room."

She groaned aloud at his story, but it wasn't responsible for the wariness she felt as they walked toward her room. Yes, protection was the issue—but not protection from strangers. The scant distance separating her and Ryan was no safeguard against her heightened awareness of him. Suddenly she felt the need to hurry, to open her motel-room door and get inside, get safe.

He was silent as she turned her key in the lock and threw open the door, turned on the light. Emboldened by her own gesture she turned to say good night. That was a mistake. Moonlight softened the sea gray of his eyes to silver. He reached across, touching her lower lip with his thumb, moving it lightly across that tender perimeter.

In that dizzy moment she knew what she had wanted all the way down the mountain and even before, through all the days and nights of correct behavior. In spite of what she'd said or decided or reasoned, she wanted his arms around her. She wanted to absorb the ready heat of his body through the layers of leather, his warmth that would contrast with the cool, sure firmness of his mouth.

As she thought this, he put his hands on her shoulders and drew her closer. Cecily felt as if her bones were melting, so that she had no strength and no resistance left. What was left was pure want, a need for his kisses and the sensuous torment of his tongue brushing open her mouth, and the thrust of its invasion. As he bent his head to hers, her head tipped back, dark lashes swooping down to veil her eyes. Yet when their lips met, his mouth was gentle on hers.

"Cecily..."

Her name on his lips was like another yearning kiss. It was as if electricity were pulsing between them, invading her senses as she waited for whatever it was he wanted to say. Ryan's eyes looked so intensely into hers that she could hardly find breath. Unable to bear even the scant distance between them any longer, she took a step toward him.

He didn't take her into his arms. Instead he pulled his hands away from her shoulders. But as if needing some contact with her still, he reached out and lightly touched her cheek. "It's been a bear of a day," he told her huskily. "Sleep well, partner."

And as he turned and left her, she thought she heard him draw a deep breath that sounded very much like a sigh.

"LOOKS LIKE a dead end up ahead," Ryan observed.

Cecily rose on her pegs and looked over his shoulder. The road they were riding on was a narrow stretch of sand that threaded between groves of pitch pine and oak. They had followed it for several miles. It had petered out to the reed-overgrown lip of a marsh. "We could double back to that other path we spotted a mile or so back," she suggested.

Ryan halted his motorcycle. "There's got to be some way of mapping this area, or else my tour will have to stick to the highway. It would be easy to get lost in this place."

"Too easy." They had left Lansing with the dawn, arriving at the coast and the pine barrens by midmorning. Since then they had branched off the main highway to explore the mazelike roads that led through acres of wilderness. A thought occurred to her. "Are we lost?"

"Probably," he answered quite cheerfully. "No problem. I've got a compass, and it'll take us to Chatsworth or Carden or one of the other towns nearby." He turned the Electra Glide. "Let's see if that other road we passed turns into a dead end, too."

"Fine with me." The trick, Cecily told herself, was to keep herself occupied. During the long ride to the barrens she had carefully schooled her thoughts and their conversation, so that the latter mostly revolved around the tour. "I wonder why the road dead-ends like this?" she wondered out loud.

"Could be one of the roads cut for stagecoaches in the early days," he told her. "There used to be quite a thriving community mining for iron."

"Iron, here?" She was surprised.

"Bog iron. People used it to make cannon for Washington's army." He paused. "Don't look now," he added softly, "but maybe one of those settlers' descendants is watching us."

A man in an old pair of jeans and a shabby Windbreaker was standing by a clump of white cedar, looking at them warily. When he took a step forward, Cecily saw that he held a wicked-looking five-tined instrument. Quickly she put a hand on Ryan's arm, and he turned to smile at her reassuringly.

"Don't worry, he's no highwayman out to rob us and drown us in the marsh, just one of the folks who lives in the barrens."

She'd heard of "pineys" who made a living off the land, and she watched with both curiosity and apprehension as the man came closer. Now she could see that under his faded red hunting cap his hair was graying, and that his weathered face and blue eyes were cautious but friendly.

"Where you folks headed for?" he called.

"We're exploring," Ryan explained. "Or we were—until we got lost and ended up here."

"This here cripple, you mean." He grinned at Cecily's astonishment, showing strong white teeth. "This here low wet place is called a 'cripple' cuz there are white cedars growing on it. Otherwise it'd be called a 'spong.'" He bent down and thrust the many-tined instrument into a large willow basket. "I've been getting me some moss."

"Sphagnum moss." Ryan sounded interested, and the elderly man nodded pleasedly.

"You're right, young fellow." He came closer to them and picked a clump of brown moss from the basket, squeezed it. Water dripped out. "See that? Florists buy this stuff because it never gets dry. My granddaddy used to tell me they used moss for bandages in Washington's time."

"Did your grandfather also live here in the barrens?" Cecily asked, and he nodded.

"His name was Hubert Gregory, same as mine. Other folks left when there was no more call for bog iron, or when they found they couldn't farm the land, but my people stayed on. Granddaddy was born right here." He paused, a trace of wariness returning to his voice. "Now what were you folks wanting in these parts?"

Cecily was surprised at the relief on Hubert Gregory's face when Ryan explained. "No fooling now. I'm not all that sure I like the idea of a crowd of motorcycles coming around here. We've got too much talk of people moving in already. But the barrens is a big place. My wife, Mary, could map you some fine trails where you'd bother nobody."

Without another word, he hefted his basket and strode away, up the path. "Should we follow him?" Cecily asked uncertainly.

"I think we've been invited to go home with him and meet Mary," Ryan replied. He dismounted from his cycle and began to walk it along the pathway after Hubert Gregory, who was waiting for them. "A map is exactly what we need."

Hubert Gregory evidently heard him, for he beamed. "My Mary can draw really fine maps. She used to teach school up near Lakewood. She's got book learning," he added with simple pride, "not like me."

His own learning was of another kind, and as they followed one narrow trail after another, he had stories to tell. The road they were on now, he said, had been cut out of the barrens for stagecoaches; it had also been the hangout of a notorious highwayman who had terrorized coaches until he was caught. "He tried to escape downriver, but they got him and hanged him right to this pine tree here, granddaddy said."

"There's a river in the barrens, too?" Hubert wagged his head at Cecily in mild disbelief.

"There sure is. You know what you want to do, the two of you? You want to take my canoe and paddle down to see Lovers' Rest. Prettier place doesn't exist anyplace."

As he spoke they took a turn in the road and came to a small sandy clearing in which stood a one-story house not much bigger than a cottage. The shingles and wood were weathered, but everything about it, from the glass in the front windows to the whitewash of the picket fence around a small flower-and-vegetable garden, had been lovingly tended. Hens cackling and a large, nondescript dog barking announced their arrival. A tall, slender woman in sun-faded jeans and a shirt rose from where she'd been weeding a patch of tomatoes.

Hubert's face practically glowed with pleasure. "Mary, here are a couple of people who want to know about the barrens. Thought I'd bring them home to meet you."

"I'm glad you did." Mary wasn't especially beautiful, but her voice had a lilt to it, and her smile tugged at Cecily's heart, for it recalled her own mother's sweetness. "I've just finished baking a pie and wishing some company would drop by." Mary went on, as she shook hands. "Hube and I don't have many near neighbors out here. Come in. Please—come in."

Inside the small house, everything looked handmade. Lovingly so, for the rag-rugs on the floor glowed with color, while the oak table Mary ushered them to had been buffed to a fine finish. "The berries come from the bog near here," Mary explained as she served her apple-cranberry pie. "You should have come a few weeks later, and you'd have seen how the bogs are flooded to get the berries."

"My mother and I used to string cranberries with popcorn for Christmas wreaths," Cecily said, then fell silent, waiting for the familiar tug of loss. She was surprised when it didn't come. Somehow, in this homey setting, remembering didn't hurt as much.

Hubert turned to his wife with a sheepish grin. "Remember when we were courting? I made you a necklace of them berries. I wished I had rubies, instead, but you said there wasn't any place to wear rubies around here."

Mary squeezed her husband's hand.

"Hube says you're looking for a map of the barrens, Ryan. Is there any special part of it you want to cover?"

Ryan shook his head. "I don't know enough about the barrens. I'll leave it to you to recommend places my tour can visit."

Going to a desk nearby, Mary drew out a large map, which she spread out on the table. "Here's where we are now," she said, tapping on the map with her finger. "I'd say if you have a day or two to spend in the barrens, you should see this area here, and this, and the river. What do you think, Hube?"

Her husband agreed.

"When Hubert said you'd mapped the area, I didn't expect something like this," Ryan said admiringly. He leaned over the detailed map, pointing out the sweep of the highway from which they had entered the barrens, the bog where they had met Hubert, the path to the Gregorys' house. "This is really a professional job."

Mary Gregory looked pleased. "I started it so I wouldn't get lost when I married Hube and came to live here. There's nearly a thousand square miles of pines here, you know, and though there are towns, too, much of the country is wild and unmarked. I was afraid someday the baby and I might get lost."

Cecily detected the slight catch in the older woman's voice, but before she could dwell on it Hubert quickly added, "With a map like this, Ryan, you and Cecily won't get lost, either."

"May I copy part of your map?" Ryan asked. But Mary wouldn't have it. "There are no copying machines around here, so I'll draw one for you. Hubert told me you want to paddle out to Lovers' Rest, and if you plan to leave the barrens by dark, you need to get down to the river." Ryan began to protest, but she shook her head firmly. "It's a pleasure to meet folks who are interested in the beauty of the barrens. We've had too much of the other kind already."

"Developers." Hubert bit down into the word as if he hated it. "There's been a few of those around here lately. They've already 'developed' thousands of acres of the barrens that isn't state owned, and now there's a company, Swindyne, Inc., that's talking of building industry up around Carden. This morning when I saw you folks, I thought you might be part of their outfit."

"One of Swindyne's goals is a plastics packaging plant," Mary added. "It sounds innocent enough, but the plant's landfill would contain waste products that wouldn't decay like normal objects. In time, rainwater would start filtering contaminants from the landfill. These would seep into underground rivers, and so on." She paused before saying somberly, "A lot of grief could come from that kind of contamination. For instance, Curene 442, a suspected carcinogen, is tied in with the plastics industry. Cancer, kidney disease, birth defects—we can do without them here in the barrens."

Cecily insisted on helping Mary clear the table. As she did so she could hear Hubert rumbling angrily on about Swindyne, Inc.

Mary sighed. "We both love the barrens, Cecily. It's a way of life to us, and it has such memories—" Breaking off, she added, "I'm glad you came by today, because otherwise it would have been a very unhappy day for Hube and me. Our only daughter, Nanci, died this day fifteen years ago from pneumonia. She was ten then. Would have been about your age if she'd lived."

"I'm sorry." There was nothing else to say, so Cecily reached out to squeeze the older woman's hand for a moment.

Mary's eyes dulled with sudden tears, yet, she still spoke briskly. "I didn't want to say anything in front of Hube. He can't bear to talk about her, he grieves so fiercely. Loving and losing tears out something in our lives, but we women can go on somehow, because there's no other choice. Men sometimes can't, and grief changes them."

Before Cecily could reply, Hubert stuck his head into the small kitchen, suggesting that his guests start at once on their canoe trip. "Daylight won't last forever," he cautioned.

Leaving their leather jackets and the motorcycle at the Gregory's, they followed Hubert around the house, then about a mile down a path so narrow that it looked more like a trail. After a quarter of a mile more, Cecily heard the murmur of running water, and soon they were pushing through clumps of low-branched trees to where a canoe had been beached beside a swift-running stream.

"It's really a glorified creek that flows off the Batso River," Hubert explained. "What you want to do now is row upstream until you come to a fork in the creek. Head right, and you'll come to some of the prettiest country God every made. Your tour will love it."

"Aren't you coming with us?" Cecily asked as Hubert helped Ryan push the canoe into the steam and then stood back. "How will we know this Lover's Rest when we get to it?"

He grinned. "I'm old enough to know when three's a crowd. Besides, you won't have any trouble recognizing Lover's Rest. When you get back, just make sure to beach the canoe good before you come on up to the house."

"He's a trusting soul," Ryan commented as Hubert started to walk away into the trees. He glanced back at Cecily. "Ready?"

Cecily viewed the canoe with suspicion. "Are you sure you can handle a canoe?"

"Canoe, kayak, sailboats, yacht—you're talking to an expert."

"Well, you're talking to a woman who can't swim. I'll go anywhere anytime on dry land, but I'm not sure about a canoe." She watched, frowning, as he held the canoe steady with one hand and reached out a hand toward her. "Anyway, what's the point? There's no way you can take your whole tour on a canoe trip."

"The purpose of this dry run is to explore all the possibilities, remember?" Sun drizzled silver into his eyes as he looked up at her. "Are you turning chicken on me?"

She didn't want to admit that it wasn't just the canoe that made her so wary. Unwillingly she let him help her into the boat. "That's the way," she heard him murmur, so close to her ear that his breath brushed her cheek, and for a moment his arm supported her back. Without the stiff barrier of leather between them, this contact of their bodies jolted her senses, made the blood surge through her as insidiuous low voltage would. Then he drew away and settled himself in the canoe behind her. "We're off."

Though the current was stong, Ryan pulled against it with such expert ease that they moved smartly along, and after a few moments Cecily relaxed and gazed into water so clear she could see the bottom. Fish swam busily in the stream; once she even saw the slow-paddling, flattened shadow of a turtle. "Probably a snapper," she exclaimed.

"Hubert said that he came up with a sixty-pound specimen one time. Luckily he saw it before it got his toes," Ryan agreed.

"Is that supposed to make me feel better?" Cecily took her eyes away from the water and looked around her, admittedly enthralled by the scenery, at least. Low overhead branches swung their broad green leaves over the water; reeds bent into the water. Seedling pines and birch and white cedars grew close enough together to form a dense curtain that seemed to enclose Cecily and Ryan in green and gold. A black-and-gold butterfly danced lazily over the water, and some distance past the fork in the stream, a pair or beavers were building a dam. The sleek creatures glared at them with almost human disapproval. Cecily couldn't resist blowing them a kiss as they paddled by.

"That's the kind of construction Hubert would approve of," she said.

"I don't doubt it." Something in Ryan's voice made her look back at him, and she was surprised to see him frowning. He went on thoughtfully, "Swindyne, Inc. and a multimillion dollar plastics packaging plant. Interesting."

"I don't think it's interesting at all. For the Gregorys' sake, I hope the corporation never makes it out here. I'd have thought it would be impractical to build any kind of plant in the barrens region."

"New Jersey is a high-tech state, and many top-level corporations, both national and international, are either based here or else they maintain a strong New Jersey presence. The undeveloped land in the barrens would certainly be tempting, and if Swindyne has acquired land here, Carden wouldn't be a bad place to build. It's accessible via the turnpike and also by the Garden State Parkway. It's out of the way, but still close enough to Trenton and other industrial areas."

He seemed about to say more but instead fell silent, and Cecily saw his eyes widen in astonishment and pleasure. Following his gaze, she saw that the waters of the stream had gentled, emptying into a small pond. The trees that surrounded the pond were giants that arched their branches over the water to form a canopy, and the silver sheen of the water was covered with dancing, dappled shadow. Clean white sand lined the lip of the pond. Farther inland, she could see the green of moss and fern interspersed with autumn flowers. Also bordered with flowers, a large, flat stone hung almost over the water's edge and formed a natural chair just big enough for two people.

"Lovers' Rest," she said with a sigh.

It was a perfect name for the place. Once they'd beached the canoe and explored the area, they found that the moss and ferns stretched on for several hundred yards, that the sand was white and soft, and the giant trees offered shade. Cecily had to agree when Ryan said, "No one would believe a place like this exists in the barrens. My tour will have to come here, which means I'm going to have to arrange for canoes. Perhaps the Gregorys will be interested in a business proposition."

She shook her head. "I'd think Hubert would want to keep the spot perfect and peaceful."

"It wasn't always peaceful. Did Mary tell you its history while you were in the kitchen?"

She shook her head, following him through the crisp carpet of moss and ferns toward the white rock.

"It's a local legend."

"Tell me," she urged. "This seems the ideal place for a story."

"It's rather a sad story, I'm afraid. It seems that during the revolution, several families came here to mine bog iron, among them the Coopers and their daughter, Hope. She was apparently quite a beauty, engaged to marry one of the wealthier men in the settlement."

"But? I know there's a 'but' someplace." Cecily sat down on the white stone and was surprised to find it slightly warm from the sun's heat. Ryan rested one booted foot on the stone. "What happened to Hope Cooper, Ryan?"

"She met a soldier in the continental army when he came out to check on the iron the army needed, and they fell in love. He didn't have much money, so the Coopers showed him the door. They locked Hope in her room, and when she protested, her father beat her."

"She should have run away!" Cecily exclaimed indignantly.

"Apparently she tried. Several times. Each time she was brought back. Finally she was married to the prosperous citizen. Shortly afterward, her soldier deserted and came looking for her. They met here at Lovers' Rest—"

"Stop."

Ryan's eyebrows arched quizzically, and she asked, "Does this have a happy ending?"

He shook his head. "They'd planned to run away together to Canada, but before they could leave Lovers' Rest, they were found. Hope's father called for her to come out, but she shouted back that she wouldn't leave her lover, that their love would last forever." There was a moment's silence before he murmured in his deep voice, "Looking at this place, I can almost believe she was right."

Cecily didn't know why the story of love and loss touched her so deeply. Perhaps because the tragedy had taken place in one of the most beautiful places she'd ever seen. Or perhaps because there were so many kinds of loss: the death of Mary's child, her own loss of her mother, Art's loss of his wife....

A hard weight seemed pressed against her heart. She tried to push away these sad memories, but it was no use. The story of lovers, centuries dead, had made Art's grief come starkly to mind. He hardly spoke of it, but she knew his pain was far worse than her own. He had lost more than wife, more than friend, more even than his heart. Cecily didn't know exactly why, but in this quiet place it was as if she could feel his tragedy more clearly than ever before.

Somewhere nearby in the trees, a bird was singing its heart out, and the beauty of the song increased the heaviness of her heart. Not wanting Ryan to see her unhappiness, she got abruptly to her feet and started to walk away from the white stone. She felt him grasp her by both her arms and pull her sharply back.

"Where are you going?" he exclaimed. "You almost walked right over those reeds into the water."

"I thought we should spend some time exploring Lovers' Rest." In spite of herself, her voice quavered.

"Are you all right?" Cecily nodded and turned away so that he wouldn't see the tears blurring her eyes. "I'm sorry if the story upset you. That tragedy happened a long time ago, Cecily."

He rubbed her arms lightly, his palms cool against her skin, and she found herself yearning toward that contact even while her better judgment warned her to pull away. Before she could do so, he had turned her gently to face him. "Why are you crying?"

She started to deny that she was, but when her eyes met his, her words trailed into silence. She had never seen such need before, or such yearning. They didn't have to speak or try to pretend. Everything she wanted to know, everything he had tried to keep from revealing, filled his eyes and spilled into his voice as he said, "I can't stand to have you sad, Cecily. You know that, don't you?"

She did know. She had felt almost since the first moment of their meeting the electricity that bonded them at some level deeper than conscious thought. Her heart began to pulse to a different tempo, a deep, steady drumbeat as he bent and brushed her cheek with his lips, his mouth lingering over her cool skin and then turning to touch her lips in the gentlest of kisses. Then again.

"I care about you. For you. I care so much...." Unfair to speak such words against her mouth, each word trembling like a separate kiss on her lips. Unfair to hold her lightly, loosely, so that she knew she had only to step backward to be free of his embrace. Crazy to freely press herself closer, lift her face to his, to curve her arms around his neck.

As Cecily moved toward Ryan, he kissed the corner of her lips, her eyelids, her chin with swift kisses that were somehow full of joyous release. She kissed him back, her mouth following the hard, lean line of his jaw, his throat, the lobe of his ear. Then, no longer gentle, his mouth took hers with a force that sucked away her breath. His tongue stroked inward, caressing, rubbing, tasting, and she met it with her own newly kindled desire. Pressed hard against him, breast to chest, hip against hip, she felt the shock waves of their shared passion jolt through her.

One hand rose to cradle her head; the other flattened against her hips, lifting her up against him. Then lovingly, possessively, his fingers relearned the outward curve of her breasts, and brushed over her shirt to find and tease the taut peaks of her nipples. She moaned with pleasure against his mouth, and he reached down and tugged impatiently at the edge of her shirt, pulling it up and out of her slacks, snapping the catch of her bra so that he could rub his fingertips over the tightly furled buds of her breasts.

Hip lips moved downward, touching, licking, caressing her throat and the vee of her shirt, then lower as buttons came away under his deft fingers. Then he was cupping her breasts in his hands, touching the coral areolas with his tongue, stroking heat through her before turning his attention once more to the aching nipples.

"Ryan...." She sighed his name as his lips fastened around her nipples. He held her tight against him as he sucked first one tender bud and then the other, and she felt the tender-tough rasp of his stubbled cheek against her softness, gloried in the seething want that his mouth and lips had awakened in her. She ran her hands over his crisp hair, his nape, trembled with the need to hurry as she pulled buttons apart from buttonholes and yanked at the buckle of his belt. "What are you trying to do to me?" she asked with a moan.

"We're doing it together." His voice was vibrant with feelings that echoed her own, and she shivered as he went down on one knee and took her with him. His mouth came back to hers, his tongue mimicking the final joining of love as they helped each other with their clothes. Her slacks followed his shirt to the ground, and he positioned them under her head as he lowered her onto the cool, fragrant ferns. Reaching up, she slid her fingers under the elastic of his dark briefs, tugged down and lifted her hips so that he could draw her lace bikinis over her thighs.

"I've wanted to touch you, kiss you like this." His mouth was busy, and so were his hands, caressing, kissing, sucking. She pressed her hands into the musculature of his back, the lean, tense waist and the powerful backs of his thighs. "I've wanted to love you for a long time."

He knelt between her legs, his body powerful in its arousal, but his lips tender as they kissed the concavity of her navel and traced erotic patterns over her thighs. They parted beneath his mind-drugging caresses.

"Love me," she whispered. "Love me, Ryan."

He came to her, poised above her on his elbows, his hipbones hard against hers. She felt herself opening to him and drawing all of him into her body and her heart, and she raised her hips to meet his first hard thrust, to welcome his body's invasion.

Cecily thought he said her name at that moment of joining, and for a moment he stayed still within her, kissing her, his mouth and touch adoring her. She kissed his hands and shoulders, licked erect the flat male nipples, gloried in his heavy fullness within her. It was she who began to move against him first, she who gasped her pleasure at the slow, deliberate strokes of his flesh in hers.

"Cecily." She saw herself reflected in the warm silver of his eyes, and though she wanted this to go on and on, she could not hold back. Ryan was her world, and Ryan was kissing her with dizzying kisses while his hard, eager body complemented her softness. And as she shattered with him, as they roared into the heart of the maelstrom together, she knew that this was where she belonged. Loving Ryan, being loved by him, was like coming home.

9

HIS ARMS were still around her. Their strength was the reality she was first aware of when the fire and the storm wind let her go. He had turned on his side and taken her with him. One brawny arm lay supporting her head, while the other curved closely around her waist. When she stretched her foot it touched his, and that tiny touch brought back all the excitement and tenderness of their coming together.

"Hello, there." Ryan kissed her, but his lips had no demand and no force, and she knew he'd been as storm tossed as she. Opening her eyes, she saw him smiling down at her. He looked contented, like a big, gray-eyed cat, and his mouth was tender.

"Hello, yourself." Cecily felt so exhilarated. She couldn't stop smiling, and she couldn't get enough of being near him. Her entire body was alive to him, to his scent, the feel of hard muscle and of smooth skin and crisp body hair. To the sweet, coolness of his mouth and the salt taste of his skin. She snuggled closer.

"Cold?" He rubbed her back lightly and sent spirals of fire curling languidly along her veins. She shook her head and pressed her cheek against his hard shoulder. "All that time wasted," he murmured. "To think I tried to live up to my promise and keep to the letter of our contract. Foolish, when it could have been like this from the beginning."

She propped herself up on her elbow and looked at him, half serious, half smiling. "I don't think so. I needed time to be with you, know you."

Dark eyebrows slanted upward. "And now you know me?" He was smiling, but the expression in those gray eyes held the hint of a challenge.

The question bothered her. She tried to focus on it and not on his nearness. On the surface, she knew Ryan to be conscientious, hardworking and fair-minded. Beyond that, she knew him as a passionate, tender lover. On the flip side of the coin, he was a man who had enjoyed tremendous wealth and power and who also enjoyed playing power games.

"Tallying up all my sins?" He was still smiling, but she wasn't sure he was teasing her.

Not caring for the seriousness of her thoughts, she drew a little away and pretended to look him over critically. "I was thinking that you're a beautiful man," she said, meaning it. Thick gold sunlight poured like honey over his broad wedge of shoulders, the hard sleekness of his waist and long, muscled legs. She ran a hand lightly along his tanned torso, even more gently over the whiteness at his hip and loins. Delicately across his thighs. "Don't laugh," she scolded him. "It's true."

Under her loving touch, she felt his want for her begin again. That gave her a sense of power and pleasure. "I'm not laughing," he assured her, and at the huskiness in his voice, she felt some deep well of pleasure and joy within her overflow with new life. "You're the one who's beautiful, my love who is like a red-gold rose." He stroked back her hair and then let the caress curve down her back and hip. "Your skin is like warm silk. You taste of honey and flowers."

His deep voice was as erotic as a poem, his sensuous touch a love song. When he kissed her breasts, she shivered with a primal longing greater than any she had felt. It seemed as if his eager mouth and stroking tongue were drawing her heart out of her. Greedily she explored his crisp hair, his shoulders and waist, the warm hardness of his manhood. His need for her was strong, but he would not satisfy her totally. Yet. Instead he continued the slow, sweet, maddening caresses.

"I've wanted to touch your breasts like this—hold them in my hands. Kiss them. Your nipples are like rosebuds." He bent lower to graze her stomach, her thighs with his mouth, then claimed her lips again with small, passionate kisses. "Do you know what it's been doing to me all morning, having you sitting against me on that motorcycle?"

Even in the midst of passion, she couldn't help a chuckle. "I do know," she told him, and he smiled at her, his eyes hazy with the same desire that sang through her blood. "I wanted you, too."

"I want you now." He drew her up and astride him and she heard his deep growl of pleasure as she took him deep. For a moment they were still...and then they began to move together.

It was as if they had always been lovers. Yet there was a sweetness that even their first lovemaking hadn't approached. They gave and took pleasure deliberately, moving and touching and kissing with a passionate tenderness, prolonging as long as they could the wondrous ecstasy of joining. And when they could no longer hold off the moment of shattering, she whispered his name again and again, until he kissed her quiet and they rested against each other, shivering and spent.

Later they lay relaxed in the sunshine among the ferns, drowsy. They stayed where they were until the sun began to disappear, and even then they didn't want to leave. It was Cecily who finally made the first move to go, saying Hubert would start worrying about his canoe.

"Good old Hubert—I'll bet he and Mary have come here, too." He sat up and drew her with him, holding her close for a long moment. She rubbed her cheek against his broad shoulders.

"You mean to make love?" He nodded, and she chuckled. "I wonder if we were that obvious."

"I doubt it. We were both too busy trying to act businesslike and professional. Are you sorry?" The question was asked softly, his lips against her cheek. She shook her head. To her surprise he let her go, and, taking her hand in his, rubbed his thumb lightly along the knuckles as if searching for the right words. "I care for you, Cecily," he told her. "Deeply. You are important to me, have been since we first met." His voice deepened. "I'm glad we found each other at Lovers' Rest."

The anxieties that had been nibbling at the edge of her mind gave way to a burst of happiness. She looked around her at the arching shadow of the trees, enjoying the fragrant, green scent of crushed grass and fern, the silvered water. The golden days of the trip seemed to stretch before them, and days and nights full of discovery and Ryan. Foolish to think beyond this golden time. Useless to think of those hours ending when she, too, had wanted Ryan from the first. Wanted him now.

"I feel that way, too," Cecily said softly. Ryan bent to kiss her again, and for a long moment they leaned against each other.

"Oh, Cecily, if we don't leave, I'll make love to you again, and then you'll be forced to make love back to me. We'll die of weakness or starvation or old age right here." With swift grace he got to his feet, pulling her with him. "Time to get back into the canoe, ma'am, but we'd better dress first. We don't want to scare the snapping turtles."

It took them some time to return to the Gregorys'. The old couple wanted them to stay and share their supper and go over the map Mary had drawn for Ryan, but though Cecily would gladly have remained longer in the relaxed and loving atmosphere of the Gregorys' home, Ryan regretfully pointed out that it would be a long ride to Lansing.

They left immediately, reaching the motel several hours later. There they found a message from Ezra Kinkaid saying Cecily's alternator had come in. Even though the next day was Sunday, the irascible mechanic added, he would consent to open his shop for work—on the assumption, of course, that he was going to charge Ryan time-and-a-half for his services.

"He means he'll charge you for my work," Cecily said. "I'll get moving first thing in the morning. And that means we'll both need a good night's sleep." She leaned into the support of Ryan's arms. "We'll both need our strength to cope with Ezra."

"I'll do my best to hold back my animal instincts." Ryan gave a tremendous yawn. "That is, if I can stay awake until we get to bed."

They slept soundly in each other's arms, to wake at dawn to renew their loving. Then they slept again and awoke refreshed and ready for the likes of Ezra.

Today he was even more cantankerous than he had been at their first meeting. Cecily had no doubt he knew his machines, and that he was a skilled mechanic. But she came close to losing her temper as he hovered near, giving unneeded advice and commenting disparagingly on her work. Finally Ryan succeeded in luring him off for a cup of coffee. To her relief and surprise, the men were gone a long time. When they returned, the mechanic was almost smiling. He checked the newly installed alternator and actually congratulated Cecily on a job well done—then floored her by adding that he thought "that young fellow Ryan" wasn't so dumb, after all, for a city boy.

"Good grief, did you brainwash him?" she asked Ryan later when they were riding out of Lansing. "I didn't think that old crab apple could crack a smile. All of a sudden he's your friend for life."

"Let's just say we found a few things in common."

"Be serious."

"He's going to be one of the mechanics in this area to carry spare parts and stand by in case my clients' motorcycles need repairs." Ryan's tone held great satisfaction. "I watched him, and he does good work. Besides, he's the kind of colorful character who would give my clients something to talk about later. It should work out well."

"So Ezra Kinkaid is actually going to work for Ryan A. Tours." Cecily shook her head. "I never figured Ezra to be the commercial type."

"Everyone likes to make money. I told you once, didn't I? Everyone has an angle."

She was aware of a small chill, as if her internal temperature had dropped. "Games again," she murmured.

"Oh, games aren't so bad." Even through the CB she could hear the husky undertone in his voice and feel her own response to it. "We can think of a few when we get to the Bramton Hotel tonight."

She was surprised. "The Bramton? I thought you'd booked rooms at the Eliott House in Trenton. Isn't that where you're supposed to have the big banquet for your tour?"

"I changed my mind when I heard about the Bramton. It's near Princeton, the brainchild of a moneyed group of entrepreneurs who want to start a chain of exclusive hotels in this part of the country. Apparently it's the prototype. I'm told the Bramton's in a class by itself, and if it's that good, I want my tour to stay there. I've booked us a suite."

He continued to talk about the hotel as they rode in the direction of Princeton. Her first glimpse of the Bramton several hours later exceeded her expectations. Instead of the ornate structure she expected, it was modern, while still exuding an aura of wealth and exclusivity. As she stopped her Harley near the wide marble steps, she had a glimpse of antique furnishings through the floor-to-ceiling chrome-and-glass doors.

"Doesn't look bad so far," Ryan said critically. He glanced around at the hotel's beautifully kept gardens and the barely visible green of the private nine-hole golf course beyond. "Still, we have to make sure. I want my clients thoroughly pampered."

A doorman, blue coat frosted with gold, came forward to ask whether they wished their vehicles parked. "I'd like to park my own cycle," Cecily said. "Is that all right?"

"Anything you want to do is more than all right," the man replied. But Ryan was frowning as they circled the hotel in the direction of a large parking lot at the rear of the building. "That doorman should have come more quickly. Service means everything in luxury hotels."

"Maybe he didn't think we were guests. I doubt if we're properly dressed for a place like this." She glanced down ruefully at her leather riding attire.

Ryan looked thoughtful as he helped her collect the baggage from the saddlebags; together they walked up the stairs of the hotel. Well-dressed men and women in business suits and sport clothes were seated around the lobby. They looked askance at Cecily and Ryan as they strolled through the electronic doors. Cecily couldn't blame them. Against the background of cream Aubusson carpets, Regency furniture and subdued lighting that brought out the colors of the artwork on the wall, she felt out of place. She found herself hanging back as Ryan stepped up to the desk.

"Sir?" A clerk had risen as they'd come in. His smile didn't quite disguise his disapproval. "Can I help you?"

Ryan's nod was a trace impatient. "You can. We wish to stay here."

The disapproval was more noticeable. "I'm sorry, sir, there are no rooms available. However, there are several other hotels I could recommend."

It was all said smoothly, politely, yet with a definite undertone of contempt. Cecily knew the people in the lobby were listening avidly as Ryan said, "The third-floor suite will do." He saw the clerk glance at his book. "You have it reserved for me."

There was a moment's pause, and then something happened to the clerk's face. His eyes opened so wide they nearly popped out of the sockets, and the flesh of his cheeks seemed to go loose like a frog's. His gasp was loud enough to carry through the suddenly still lobby. "Mr. Alexander?"

Ryan nodded silently.

"Mr. Alexander, I didn't recognize— Of course the suite is ready for you and Ms Leeds, sir." He turned sharply to the bell captain. "Take Mr. Alexander's and Ms Leeds's bags up to the suite at once," he hissed.

Ryan turned to Cecily. "Do you want to stay?"

Everyone was watching them, and she was becoming embarrassed. "What do you want to do?"

"I haven't decided." His face was hard, his eyes as cold as gray ice as he turned back to the clerk. "My clients will be in riding leathers, too. I want them welcomed, not treated like pariahs. To treat someone badly just because of outward appearance is inexcusable."

She hadn't thought it possible, but she was feeling sorry for the clerk. He looked ready to cry. She put a hand gently on Ryan's arm. "We all make mistakes, Ryan."

The look the clerk turned on her was one of pure gratitude, and Ryan's eyes softened. "So you think we should give the Bramton a chance?"

Before she could speak, there were hurried footsteps behind them. A man cleared his throat. Turning, Cecily looked into a stranger's florid face; the clerk melted away. "Mr. Alexander—Ms Leeds, my name's Roger Swinton. I'm one of the owners of the hotel. I'd like to welcome you to the Bramton, and I hope you'll allow us to serve you in any way possible."

Ryan shook the eagerly proffered hand, though his expression remained watchful. "Mr. Swinton," was all he said, and after a moment Roger Swinton spoke again.

"My apologies for this regrettable incident. The clerk's a fool. If he'd had any brains at all, he would have realized you and Ms Leeds might arrive on motorcycles." He paused before adding, "We'll do everything in our power to make up for our error."

"That's fair," Ryan conceded.

Roger Swinton looked vastly relieved, and Cecily marveled that Ryan Alexander's goodwill and custom meant so much to this luxurious hotel. "Your bags will be taken up immediately. In the meantime—perhaps a drink in the bar to refresh you? No? Then perhaps an aperitif later. We serve from six to ten. You'll be seated whenever you're ready." He almost bowed as he turned away.

Cecily stared at the man's departing back. "Talk about an attitude change," she murmured. "Or, as George would say, chickens one day—feathers the next."

"I always knew George Zolichick was a wise man." At the odd note in his voice, she glanced up at him, and saw him watching the retreating Swinton. "There really was no attitude change here. Money talks loudly in places like this."

For once she had to wholeheartedly agree with this statement. As two bellhops carried their baggage to the elevators, she caught snatches of conversation alluding to vacations in Majorca and Puerto Vallarta, hints of the acquisition and dispensing of millions of dollars of stock. Even the jogging suit one of the guests was wearing had to cost more than Leeds Motorcycles took in in a week.

As for the suite Ryan had booked, it took up nearly half the third floor. There were two bedrooms opening into an elegant sitting room decorated in whites and browns and almond, brightened with exquisite floral arrangements and made elegant by sculpture and paintings that even her inexpert eye could see were valuable originals.

Ryan was walking around taking inventory. "Two separate bathrooms, not bad." Two bedrooms—this one is done in pink and white, so it must be yours." He looked critically around as silent employees set down the bags and slipped away. "Not bad," he repeated, testing the plush, white carpet with the toe of his boot and surveying white couches of softest leather, complemented by the rich dark glow of fine rosewood furniture. "Let's look at the rest of the setup."

The bathrooms were magnificent. No other word for it, Cecily thought. The one nearest Ryan's regal bedroom was done in white and was strictly masculine. It boasted a square sunken tub of creamy marble, a Jacuzzi and a sauna. In an adjacent dressing area, Nautilus equipment was arranged.

Her bathing area was luxury of another kind, with pink carpets setting off pale-pink marble and translucent plastic so fine it resembled mother-of-pearl. Orchids and ferns in wicker pots were arranged around the sunken tub, and crystal atomizers offered perfume: Jean Charles Brosseau, Chanel, Dior.

"That's all right, then," Ryan said once she had thoroughly approved the bathroom and the comfortable bedroom beyond, with its king-size bed and ankle-deep plush carpet.

They were interrupted by a waiter bringing up a silver tray of coffee, tea and French pastries. There was also a note from Roger Swinton to Ryan.

"He wants us to be his guests at dinner," he told her, folding the note thoughtfully. "It seems the other two owners of the hotel are in town, and they'd like to meet and talk. What do you think?"

"It would be a good chance for you to go over your tour," she suggested.

"Not 'me,' 'we.'" He caught her hands and swung her into his arms. Again she felt the hot shiver of desire fill her blood. "We're a team, remember?"

Remembering their earlier treatment by the clerk, she hesitated, but it was hard to think while his mouth nibbled at her lower lip and the lobe of her ear. As he kissed her in delicious places, she said, "I only packed one dress, Ryan. I didn't think we'd come any place this grand. And I'm not much on making polite conversation with millionaires. I don't think I'd do your tour justice."

"You'd always do me proud." His mouth found hers, stopping her next protest. After a moment he drew away. "I'd like nothing more than to say to hell with Swinton and his friends and stay here with you, but tonight's important. There are arrangements to be made about the tour—we'll need to discuss parking facilities for the motorcycles, for instance."

She sighed. "Do I have the time to take a very long, uninterrupted soak?"

She had seen baths like this before in movies and in magazines, but she had never bothered to wonder what it felt like to wallow in such luxury. She'd been positive she would never have a chance to try one out. Now as she carefully unpacked her one dress, then undressed and walked naked across the thick carpet to the water, she felt gloriously frivolous, deliciously sinful. The warm, caressing water welcomed her like a lover's arms. She closed her eyes and let the lapping, scented water enfold her. This was living. The kind of living a woman could easily get used to.

"How's the water?"

Ryan was standing in the bathroom doorway. He wore only a towel knotted around his lean waist, a white contrast to his tanned body. His eyes slid over her, and against the light kiss of water she felt her nipples tauten and harden. "I'd find out for myself," he went on, "but you did specify an 'uninterrupted' soak."

"A woman's entitled to change her mind…."

Useless to deny her response when she could feel the warm honey stealing through her pulse at the sight of him. In the intensely feminine bathroom he looked big, supremely male. When he dropped his towel and walked to the edge of the tub, her roving eyes took in the strength of his need for her.

She moved to accommodate him as he entered the water, but he didn't let distance separate them for long. Quickly her soft, firm breasts were pressed against him. He licked droplets of water from her cheek, then rubbed his mouth against hers lightly. "Water's fine," he murmured against her ear. "Now to make sure I approve of its effect on you."

"I'm not sure I should approve of any of this." She sighed, then giggled as he ran his fingers over her back and ribs in a tickling motion, sighed again as the teasing became a caress.

"But you enjoy it. It's important to enjoy." His eyes were slits of light and pleasure. "I think I'm getting your feedback about this bath, Ms Leeds, and I like what I'm getting." Lightly, as delicately as the movement of the water that surrounded them, he stroked her breasts, teased her nipples. Then lifted her so that he could take the coral buds into his mouth. Sucking, licking, flicking at them with his tongue as his hands roved lower, exploring the secret places of her body.

"You know that we'll be late for dinner," but her words weren't a protest. She cared nothing for anything else, certainly not for Roger Swinton and his friends, while Ryan delicately teased the satin secrets of her thighs, while his mouth tormented her breasts, her throat, her lips. Greedy for more kissing and for more of his touch, she pressed herself against him and got lost in the erotic slide of wet skin against wet flesh. Her hands explored his furred chest, the long lean legs, the strength of his thighs and his arousal. She was almost mad to touch more, to press closer, to meld with him, and when he lifted her astride his knees, she felt buoyant in the water, free.

Then there was no sensation except the delicious, magic friction of their coming together. Their lips clung; their hands caressed. Her body welcomed him, enclosed his hard readiness. They moved languidly at first, but gradually with stronger, harder strokes. Rippling like the water. Hotter than the water. Rising harder, faster, until they were spinning in a whirlpool, rocking against each other. And as she clung to him, two words formed unbidden in her half-numbed mind. *My love,* she thought. *Ryan, my love.*

LATER CECILY WAS CONVINCED that there was magic in Ryan's touch. Tonight the servicable green wool-and-polyester-blend dress she had packed seemed to flow round her like emerald silk, the colors bringing out the color of her eyes, emphasizing the curving slenderness of her figure. When she met Ryan in the suite's sitting area some time later, his eyes told her she was beautiful.

He himself appeared elegant in a dark-gray Italian silk suit and fine-tailored linen shirt, all impeccably pressed by the hotel staff. They made a handsome couple. She saw that thought in the eyes of the Bramton's other guests; noted, too, that many of the women eyed Ryan with open interest. When they reached the lobby, Roger Swinton and two other men were waiting for them. Roger introduced the tall, balding man as Charles Cardyne of Cardyne Enterprises, and the younger, intense one as Oliver Ames Hartwell, president of the New Jersey Bryant Bank.

Swinton suggested a drink in the Atrium Bar before dining, and Cecily was delighted with the intimate room. The glass walls exposed a magnificent atrium and swimming area. The lighting in the bar was soft, the subtle music soothing. Swinton looked pleased when she told him so. "I'm glad you like it, and I hope you're enjoying your stay at the Bramton."

She assured him that she was, to which Ryan agreed. "I've been getting excellent feedback from my associate," he said, deadpan.

Expecting them to continue talking about Ryan A. Tours and the Bramton, Cecily was surprised when the conversation turned general. Charles Cardyne enjoyed motorcycle racing and had seen Arthur Leeds race. The banker, Hartwell, spoke of the multinational corporations that were becoming successful in New Jersey. And Roger brought the talk around to the Raya department-store chain, admiring a new and exclusive line of Chinese silk that had been an instant success.

Finally the intense young banker leaned forward. "I have to confess to being curious. What really brings you here, Mr. Alexander? We hoped, naturally, that you were interested in our consortium."

As if this were some sort of signal, the other two men leaned forward. Cecily could sense the tension gripping them all, but to her the drama was unfathomable. "I'm not interested in hotels, gentlemen," Ryan was saying. "But I am very much interested in Swindyne, Inc."

"Dammit, I told you so," Cardyne exclaimed excitedly. "I knew it had to be talk about our proposed industrial development that brought you here."

"Swindyne." Cecily didn't realize she'd spoken aloud until four pairs of eyes turned to her. "You're the company that wants to build a plastics packaging plant near Carden?"

Roger Swinton nodded. "You're well-informed, Ms Leeds, but of course you would be." He turned to Ryan, adding, "Apart from the obvious profit to Swindyne, our project means jobs, economic growth, a better way of life for many people in the Carden area."

Oliver Ames Hartwell put the tips of his fingers together and rubbed his chin with them. "The question is, in what way you are interested in us, Mr. Alexander? Bluntly speaking, we are interested in you. Your name on our corporate board of directors would be of great benefit to Swindyne. On the other side of the coin, we'd be a sound investment for you."

"I don't dispute that. I realize Swindyne's a young and aggressive corporation, and that your stock has increased twenty cents a share for the third quarter this year. I'm impressed by you, and I've wanted to meet you." Ryan broke off as a waiter silently placed a second round of drinks on the table. Cecily was experiencing the first faint stirrings of horror. She was beginning to see what the men were talking about.

Surely not, she told herself. Remembering the quiet beauty of the barrens, remembering Lovers' Rest, Ryan couldn't be saying what she thought he was saying. Not when he was smiling at her like that. "As I told you, I'm more than interested. I'd like to go into depth about your development later—perhaps tomorrow morning?"

"Wait, Ryan, please." Not content to let the matter drop so quickly, she turned to the three members of Swindyne. "Don't the people who live in the barrens object to having you build a processing plant that could be damaging environmentally?"

The men looked at one another; Oliver Ames Hartwell shrugged. "Environmental groups have protested, of course, but we're confident we'll reach some kind of compromise. Our engineers report that there's no danger to the ecology of the area, for one thing; and for another the barrens are pretty much deserted, made up of swamps and sand and a few cranberry bogs. Much of the area is crying out for development. As they say, 'The dogs bark, but the caravan moves on.'"

"People aren't dogs."

"And the issues aren't quite so cut and dried as you make them." Ryan's voice held a warning note; obviously he didn't like her opposition. She didn't know which hurt more, the fact that Ryan was siding with a group that would change life in the barrens, or the knowledge that even now, after all they had shared, he was back to playing his games. Except that now the stakes were as high as a way of life for people they both knew.

Her voice held a barely discernible tremor as she said, "The issue seems very clear to me. You're interested in joining Swindyne, even though by doing so you'll be helping to destroy the Gregorys' way of life."

She held his eyes, willing him to remember, but instead of softening, the sea-gray eyes hardened. Roger Swinton laughed. "Your associate can get pretty dramatic," he commented.

Ryan's laugh was a little rueful. "Cecily's used to being dramatic in her line of work. Once she had to help me wrestle over eight hundred pounds of motorcycle upright. She's been invaluable to me during this trip." He was smooth, and he was good, she thought bitterly. And he was used to directing the talk where he wanted it to go. Now he was watching her expectantly, confidently, sure she would pick up her cue.

All she had to do to end this awkward moment was change the subject, talk about the tour or about Art's racing. All he wanted her to do was play the game as he wanted it to be played. She looked at him unhappily, and was astonished to see an odd expression in his eyes. Ryan seemed almost to be pleading with her to understand his position.

That took her aback, and she could only stare at him. Supposing joining Swindyne was important to him, and he was asking for her help? What would it hurt if she went along with him? Nothing would change. She could no more stand in the way of Swindyne than she could fly to the moon. Her acceptance wouldn't make a tad of difference, whereas her defiance might hurt Ryan. She didn't want to do so, and yet as the thought filled her mind, she recalled Mary Gregory's speaking quietly about the loss of her child, and about the barrens, which were so dear because they held the memory of her daughter.

That snapped the deadlock. Cecily couldn't fight the consortium, true, but she didn't have to stay here and listen and approve their plans. "Perhaps we can talk about our adventures on the road another time," she said, getting to her feet. "At the moment, I'm very tired. Would you excuse me, please?"

She had a quick look at their faces: Roger Swinton was surprised; Cardyne, sardonic; the young banker, thoughtful. She didn't look at Ryan, but as she stepped away from the table, she heard his step behind her.

"Cecily." His deep voice made her turn, even though she didn't want to. "Look, I know you've had a long day, but dinner with these men is important for many reasons." He would have gone on but she'd had enough.

"I'm sorry, I can't smile and be charming while you cozy up to Swindyne. In Whitwater you said you disagreed with your father's environmental policies, but I suppose its expedient to forget that, now that you stand to make a profit by helping to pollute the barrens."

It was as if a light had gone out. All traces of empathy or understanding or caring were wiped from his face. She could have been looking into the cold eyes of a stranger. "You seem to have it all worked out. But you're forgetting something, aren't you? You're still working for me."

Her own anger rose in response to his hard tone. "I work for you on the road. It's not part of my contract to help you make your million-dollar deals that destroy people." She paused, then added bitterly, "What hurts most is that you set all this up. You recognized the name 'Swindyne' the moment Hubert said it, didn't you? That was why you insisted on coming to the Bramton. You wanted to meet Swinton and Cardyne and Ames, but you couldn't be honest about it. 'Use them before they can use you,' isn't that right?"

Without another word, he turned and went back to the waiting men. As Cecily walked out of the bar, her insides were clenching like impotent fists. An ache of sadness and hurt rippled through her, together with an anger she directed at herself. She had known what he was like. She had known they were poles apart. From the beginning it had been perilous to care for a man to whom life meant power and money and the games played to attain them. She did care; that was the trouble. The corrosive pain within her told her how much she cared. She felt so much for Ryan that a few minutes ago she had been ready to compromise everything she knew was right, play his game so that he would continue to be her lover.

She didn't like what she'd found out about herself, but at least she was being honest. At least she knew what she had to do. "I have to get away from him," Cecily whispered. "I have to go home right now."

10

HOME. Cecily forced all other thought out of her mind as she dialed the familiar Clinton number on the exquisite white-and-gold phone in the suite. There seemed to be a cavity somewhere deep in her heart, an empty space that found its echo in the huge empty suite. Only the thought of home and the people there kept her steady.

She wanted to be in the shop. She could almost smell the grease and the rust and exhaust fumes, almost hear George arguing with Art in the office under the dusty photographs. The whir and click of the dial tone made her impatient. Surely it was still early enough for Art to be in the shop. He never quit before seven or eight.

The male voice that answered the phone was unfamiliar, and for a moment she was sure she'd dialed the wrong number. Then she heard Art's muffled voice in the background. "This is Cecily," she said. "Who is this?"

"Jon—Jon Simonson. I work here afternoons. How's the trip coming?" he went on eagerly. "We've been reading about you in the papers over here. The Globe did a big feature article on Leeds Motorcycles and another one on Ryan A. Tours just this week. You're a celebrity."

Before she could ask a question, Jon was gone, and Art was speaking excitedly over the wires. "Ceci, how are you?"

"I'm fine. And you?" Art was obviously more than fine. There was a lilt to his voice she hadn't heard in years. He sounded more like the old Arthur Leeds who had raced all over the world.

"Everything's going well here, Ceci. In fact, I hired us a part-time assistant. Nice boy, good with his hands, real dependable. Hope you don't mind."

"I'm relieved! I've been worried about your doing all that work alone." She waited for Art to deny that any amount of work was too much for him, but to her surprise he agreed with her.

"There's been much too much work for us to handle on our own. Ceci, you wouldn't believe the shop. It's like the world suddenly discovered Leeds Motorcycles."

She asked what he meant, and he explained that since the news of her trailblazing expedition with Ryan had hit the media, people had been beating a path to the small shop in Clinton.

"The *Globe* article was the icing on the cake," Art said a shade smugly. "That fellow Leonard Coxe was right. A whole lot of people think the world of whatever Ryan Alexander does. And now that Ryan's hired us, the glamour's rubbed off. What's more, apart from buying cycles, a lot of them are practically begging me to teach them to ride and race. When you get back, we'll sit down and talk about starting a school. You remember we used to talk about it."

"Won't that cost money?"

"No problem. Even that pessimist George agrees. Banks are practically rolling over and begging Leeds Motorcycles to borrow money from them. All we have to do is find a suitable track and start a real school." Art's voice almost quavered with eagerness. "We'll call it the Leeds School of Motorcycle Riding. Or maybe I should call it after you. We wouldn't be doing so well if you hadn't taken the job with Ryan."

Cecily didn't like the coldness that was growing inside her. As she listened to the happy tone in her father's voice, she wondered what would happen if she severed her bond with Ryan.

Nothing much would happen to Ryan. He would get some other expert easily enough, here in Princeton or in Trenton. Yet if she quit him, for no matter what reason, people would think Ryan had let her go because her services weren't satisfactory. And what would that do to Art's dreams?

"We're doing well because we're good," she said, more to herself than to Art.

"Sure we are, but nobody knew that until Ryan came along. I'm telling you, Cecily, that man's a godsend." Art lowered his voice. "I haven't told you the best news of all. I've been invited to go to England."

"To England!" she exclaimed, and he gleefully told her that a cyclist club in Boston had asked him to advise them on a proposed tour of the British Isles.

"Of course they say they're interested because I raced in England and on the Isle of Man, but it's really because Ryan A. Tours hired us. Naturally I told them you were my partner and had to come along, so they agreed to fly us both to London. What do you think?"

By the time she hung up the phone, Cecily felt as if she'd been gutted and left to dry in the sun. She walked to the window of the suite and looked out on the now-dark cityscape lit by thousands of yellow electric eyes. There was no choice and no retreat. There was no chance of her quitting Ryan's employ and going home. She would have to stick it out, unless—

Unless Ryan himself let her go. She hadn't thought about it, but he had been furious with her tonight. Was he angry enough to fire her? She almost wished he would, even though that would mean the end of Art's dreams. Her problems would be solved then.

She moved back from the window, banging her shin against a rosewood desk as she did so. The sharp pain brought tears to her eyes. With the pain came an overwhelming need to escape these elegant surroundings, which were not part of her world, but Ryan's. She would take a walk. She would walk and try to think and put everything into perspective.

Limping to her bedroom, Cecily changed into her jeans, and as she drew out a sweater from her baggage, her journal fell onto the floor. She picked it up and was returning it to its place in her bag, when her eye fell on a few lines written after Lovers' Rest. Tender lines about the magic of the place and the magic of Ryan's arms. She stuffed the notebook out of sight into her bag, remembering Art's reference to Leonard Coxe. She hoped Mr. Coxe wouldn't be too upset that the article on Ryan's "secret soul" would never be written—not by her, anyway. In fact, the less she thought of Ryan the better.

It took her a few minutes to change into her sweater and take the elevator down to the main lobby, but she hadn't realized it would be so cold. She gasped as she gulped air into her lungs, and thought that this was even better—a bracing walk around the block would do her a world of good. But it was a deceptively long block, and the night was not only cold but dark, and the street more or less empty. She had just decided to turn back, when she heard footsteps behind her.

She turned, saw nobody. Could it have been her imagination? No, for now the footsteps echoed nearer. Whoever was following her was in a hurry, and she began to walk more swiftly. Then, as she turned the corner, there was a loud clattering and clanging. She gasped, tensing to run, and at the same moment Ryan's familiar voice spoke out of the dark.

"Don't panic—you just knocked over a trash can. Where are you going in such a hurry?"

Relief made her dizzy. "Why didn't you call out if you knew it was me? What are you doing out here, anyway? I thought you'd still be talking with Swindyne, Inc."

"I didn't know it was you until you cried out." His voice had that hard edge to it. "Didn't it occur to you that it mightn't be exactly safe to go for a stroll in the dark?"

The shadow thrown up behind him made him loom larger than life, and when he took a step closer she had to force herself not to back away. "So your 'tiredness' was just an excuse," he said.

Was he going to fire her? She felt a rush of fighting spirit. If speaking frankly would cost her her job, so be it. "I saw no point in staying," she snapped. "If you want to cancel our agreement after tonight, I'll understand perfectly."

"Swindyne has nothing to do with your contract with Ryan A. Tours."

The chill of Ryan's voice permeated her bones to a degree beyond mere physical cold. Was she relieved or disappointed? Before she could analyze her feelings, he said, "Tomorrow you'll meet with Roger Swinton and arrange for parking for the tour's motorcycles, as well as consult with him about available service for the machines." The harsh precision of his words was at variance with his usual, easy way of talking, so that she knew he was seething. "I have a business meeting with Swindyne in the afternoon. It will probably last through the evening, so you and I will leave the hotel the day after tomorrow. Once we start down the Atlantic coast, we'll be on the last leg of our New Jersey trip, before the turnaround point near Camden."

"I'll be ready to leave." Since there was no more to be said, Cecily began to walk away from him, down the dark street toward the hotel.

"Wait a minute." Even here, even now, his deep voice had the power to turn her breathless, and involuntarily she stopped. "You're not even dressed properly," he said, and before she realized what he was doing, he had unbuttoned his suit jacket and draped it across her shoulders. It carried his scent, the feel of him. "I can't have you catching pneumonia at this late date. Journey's end isn't so far away."

He was concerned about the rest of his tour. That was his primary goal, and always had been. Whatever else had happened meant little or nothing to him. Well, she thought, to the devil with him.

Meeting his gaze squarely, she removed his coat and handed it back. "Don't worry about me. I can take care of myself."

The gray eyes looking down into hers were suddenly shuttered, as if a curtain had come down. "Understood," Ryan said.

THEY SPENT ANOTHER DAY at the Bramton, then began the long ride down the Atlantic coastline. Indian summer had given way to cold drizzle. Fog swept up from the Atlantic ocean and chilled them both, until they swung inland again to reach the halfway point near Camden.

Here Ryan had arranged for comprehensive media coverage, and they spent a half-hour in front of TV cameras on a New Jersey network talk show, an hour afterward talking to news reporters and posing for photographs. Various sports, news and business magazines were represented, and Cecily got an education, listening to Ryan being interviewed. She finally understood what Leonard Coxe had been up against when he'd asked for an in-depth article on Ryan for *Intro*, for though Ryan appeared to answer every question frankly, he always shifted away from anything that could be considered personal.

She found herself falling back on this ploy when questioned about intimate details of her trip with Ryan. She wasn't as skilled at evasion as Ryan, but she managed, until a feature writer for a New York daily asked her how it felt to work for one of the most influential young entrepreneurs in the country. "Would you care to comment on the talk about

Ryan Alexander and Swindyne, Inc.?" he asked. "It's been rumored that your boss was the one who sent Swindyne back to the drawing board."

Cecily wasn't sure she'd heard right. "Sent Swindyne back to the drawing board? You mean on the industrial developments in the pine-barrens area near Carden?"

The reporter confirmed this. "That development has had its controversial aspects, but Swindyne has a lot of clout in state and local government. It seemed certain the firm was going to go ahead and build—over a lot of objections by environmental protection groups. Then suddenly they pulled back, and it's rumored that they're 'rethinking.' The question is, did Ryan Alexander have something to do with this move?"

"I...think you'd better ask him about that." Surely there was some mistake? There had to be. Ryan hadn't been feigning his interest in joining Swindyne.

To her surprise, Ryan didn't deny the reporter's question when it was turned on him. "I think you're crediting me with too much influence," he said. "All I did was discuss the idea with Swindyne's board of directors and make a few observations. I'm sure that whatever decision the corporation made was their own."

She wasn't sure what that decision was, and in view of what had happened at the Bramton, she wasn't sure she ought to ask. Curiosity got the better of her, however, and she put the question to him later as they were riding toward the Bear Mountains on the first leg of their homeward journey.

He seemed to hesitate before answering. "What I told the press was true," he then said. "I went over

Swindyne's entire project with them and pointed out some problems that were sure to occur. I made alternate suggestions that would provide an industry that would be both 'clean' and profitable, a project, in fact, that I'm interested in joining as an investor."

That made no sense. "But you seemed so interested in their plastics packaging plant. . . ."

"I knew their type of industrial development would be wrong for that particular area, and I convinced them of it—not through emotional outpourings about the beauty of nature, but in black-and-white terms of profit and loss. I knew I had to see the plans and figures before I could prove my point logically."

He had meant to dissuade Swindyne all along. She was so stunned by what he'd just said that she missed seeing a rut in the road. She hardly felt the jolt. "You went to the Bramton to protect the barrens. Why didn't you tell me so?"

"I didn't know for sure how things would work out. Besides, people usually believe what they want to." His voice over the CB was cool, dismissive. "Best to watch the road. It gets rough around here. You don't want to get into an accident on the way home."

Cecily didn't answer, but concentrated harder on the road. The sun was strong with the first warmth they'd had for days. Though she felt the heat of it on the back of her leather jacket, she was oddly chilled. She knew he hadn't bothered to tell her about her mistake because he felt she should have trusted him. Because she should have known him enough to realize— But, she thought unhappily, how could she know Ryan? He was like a diamond, full of facets of light and darkness. He was hard; he was tender; he could be understanding or inflexible. The more she knew about him, the less she knew.

"Anyway, the Gregorys' way of life is safe," she murmured, and realized she'd left the CB switched on when he swiftly replied.

"Until another firm comes along with another plan to make money. Sorry, Cecily, but like it or not, those are the facts."

"Life goes on. Tide and time stop for no man. Is that it?"

"Something like that." Though today she rode ahead of him she could feel the cool sea gray of his eyes on her back and the intensity of that regard. It made her uncomfortable. "You're too softhearted for your own good."

There was something in his voice that changed the quality of her tension. Electricity began to hum along her veins, emphasizing the emptiness she had felt since Trenton. "We'll be crossing through some of the loveliest countryside in New Jersey today," he was saying in a brisk businesslike voice, "and I want my clients to have as good a trip going home to Boston as they had coming."

"Do you think I wouldn't be aware of that?" she asked indignantly, and he replied at once.

"No, you'd be very aware." She was dismayed at how quickly his praise could lift her spirits. "That's why I came to Leeds Motorcycles in the first place."

And that, she thought, was the pure and unvarnished truth. He was her boss—that was all he was. She should be grateful he had redefined the reason for her being there. The problem was that no matter what, she was drawn to him. Even now, while she drove ahead of him through rolling hills and valleys that were gold and green velvet in the late-afternoon sun, she was thinking not of the road but of Ryan.

He kept muscling into her mind. She didn't want him there. Their ways of life were poles apart. She should have obeyed her instincts and avoided getting involved with him from the first.

"You seem tired. Do you want me to take the lead?" His voice over the CB startled her, and she realized how deeply she'd been immersed in thought. "We'll be riding against the sun as we climb the hill."

It was like Ryan to want to take the lead, but for once she felt stubborn. "I'm fine," she insisted.

Her visor screened out a little of the sun's dazzle as they climbed the side of a gently rolling mountain, giving her the sensation of climbing into fire. The memory of Lovers' Rest filtered through the protective barriers of her mind, and suddenly she was afraid. Couldn't she ever stop thinking of Ryan? Would every tranquil river and every twisting mountain road remind her of him? She rebelled against the idea, but it stayed with her as she took a curve. Both her preoccupation and the glare of late sunlight stopped her from reacting in time to the thick, leafy branch that had fallen across the entire width of the road.

As Cecily called a warning to Ryan over the CB, she fought panic. On this narrow mountain stretch there was no safety exit, no way of avoiding the enormous branch. She couldn't hope to stop in time—the branch was less than fifty feet ahead of her, and she would need at least seventy feet of braking distance. The only way to avoid a crash was to steer into the thick trees growing along both sides of the path, but that was dangerous and would surely lead to injury. She hit her rear brakes and began to pump the front brakes to gear down. She knew braking on a turn was dangerous, but there was no choice.

"Don't lock the front brakes, Cecily. Lean—lean to the right." As she braked, she heard Ryan's voice over the CB. "To the right," he repeated loudly.

She leaned right. This would help her stop, keeping her from skidding, but she wasn't slowing down fast enough. She saw the branch clearly as it came rushing toward her, the thick, evil-looking trunk of it twisted and gnarled, the spreading leafy-green and brown of the smaller branches and twigs toward the top. They seemed to reach out to grab at her like a witch's hand. She was going to hit it. She was going to hit—

All of a sudden Ryan was passing her on her extreme right, heading directly for the branch. There was a whoosh of sound, a splintering of branches, and then, miraculously, he was through. Acting instinctively, she threw her whole concentration into following him at the exact point of his entry. Then branches were clawing at her leathers, her helmet, and she smelled the acrid crushed leaves and bleeding bark.

Shaking like a drunk, Cecily's Sportster bucked and slid as it hit ruts on the shoulder of the road. She was fighting for control when she heard Ryan talking to her. "You're through now. It's all right, Cecily. You're okay."

He was right. Her motorcycle was slowing, stopping. She leaned over her handlebars, trying to catch her breath. The next minute she felt his hands on her shoulders. "Are you hurt?" he asked urgently.

She shook her head.

"Sure?"

He was bending over her, his visor pushed back up onto his forehead, his face pale and streaked with sweat and dirt. She'd never seen such stark fear in his eyes before. Responding to it, she managed a whisper. "My fault. I wasn't as alert as I should have been coming around that turn. I—I didn't see that branch quickly enough, and then I geared down too fast." She smelled once more the green scent of bruised tree branches and shivered. "But you. You took a terrible chance."

"I saw that the branches thinned out at a certain point, that's all." The fear was leaving his eyes, and his grip eased on her shoulders. He smiled at her. "I'll bet Art Leeds had this happen to him once or twice in his career."

Cecily looked at the thickly wooded sides of the road, then back at the branch. "If you hadn't been there, I'd have broken my cycle and a few bones, at least."

"Weren't you the one who said partners had to watch out for each other on the way?" He gave her a small, bracing shake, and the warmth of his touch seemed to transmit itself through her leather jacket. "All right now?"

"Yes." She trembled inwardly, as if some chain reaction was starting to build deep within her, and she stilled it with effort. She'd almost done one stupid thing today; she wasn't going to fall apart now.

"I'd like to be off this mountain road before twilight," he was saying. "I'd hoped to reach the Hudson River tonight, but we'll stop at a motel along the way." He gave her a searching look. "Will you be all right if we ride?"

She nodded, and he took the lead. She was grateful that she was alert and in control, even more grateful when another hour of riding brought them, at twilight, to a small town and an almost-deserted motel. It was small, unpretentious and badly in need of paint. Cecily said, "It's not the Bramton."

Ryan agreed. "But I've slept in worse. Remind me to tell you about the night I spent in a woodcutter's hut up near the Tibetan border. Cold as hell outside, smoky and infested with lice inside...."

"Remind me never to ask." She shuddered, and he laughed.

"There even seems to be a snack bar attached to the motel. Comforts of home. We could both do with something hot."

The menu was limited, so they ordered hamburgers and soup. Cecily's stomach rebelled against the greasy, oversalted stuff. She also found she was suddenly exhausted, and leaving Ryan to discuss with the motel owner the best way of reaching the Hudson River, she went to her room. There she shed her clothes and stepped into the shower stall.

She didn't know exactly how it happened. One moment she was standing under the warm, soothing streams of water; in the next moment she was hurtling into terror. It was as if she were back on the mountain road, that huge branch rushing toward her. She was powerless to stop herself from reliving every terrible second of that encounter, and something in her mind screamed that she could have died on the mountain. She could have easily smashed herself and her Sportster against the trees. She would never have seen Art again, never again felt the wind or smelled the rain or gone home. Another thought formed, unbidden. She could never have been with Ryan again.

A whimper forced its way from between her clenched teeth. Cecily tried to shake off this living nightmare, tried to stop herself from thinking any further, but she couldn't. Nor could she stop shaking. She was trembling so violently that her teeth chattered. She could hardly manage to shut off the water and wrap herself in a towel before creeping into her bed. There she huddled under the covers like a wounded thing.

Even then the terrible images came, even faster. The mountain road, the enormous branch, the skidding motorcycle and the blinding sun— This time she was going down, down into the dark, and even Ryan couldn't help her, even though she could hear his voice in the distance. Nobody could help her.

"Cecily?" It was Ryan's voice again, but nearer this time. It filtered through the chaotic images in her mind. He was knocking on the door. "Are you all right in there?" he shouted. "I thought I heard you call out."

Ryan was there. She wanted, needed the comfort of his arms. Forcing herself out of bed, she made her way across the room to the door. It took such a long time for her shaking body to obey her that she was afraid he'd be gone by the time she managed, but when she pulled open the door he was still there. She was so relieved that tears filled her eyes.

When he saw her face, he came and shut the door. Lifting her in his arms, he carried her to a chair by the bed and sat cradling her shaking, towel-wrapped body against his. She was too upset to register anything but the reassurance of his arms around her, but some part of her consciousness took in the fact that he, too, had bathed. The bare skin of his throat was slightly damp against her cheek, and he wore a sport shirt pulled hastily over jeans.

She felt the warm hardness of his bare foot against her own ice-cold one as he said, "It's all right, Cecily, I'm here." He crooned the words deeply, spoke them as tenderly as if she were a child awakened from nightmares.

"I—I don't know what's wrong with me," she mumbled. "I was fine. And then I st-started to shake and couldn't stop."

He was stroking her tumbled hair. "Delayed shock. I should have suspected something like this was coming when you were so exhausted this evening. It wasn't just normal fatigue."

"C-can't be," she protested. He shifted her weight so that he could hold her more comfortably against him. Beneath her cheek she heard the steady beat of his heart.

"Take my word for it, it happens this way sometimes. I remember when I fell down the side of a chasm on the Matterhorn. There was a bad storm blowing at the time, and I was sure I was a dead man. I dangled on a rope for an hour before the people with me managed to pull me up." His strong, competent hand rubbed her stiff shoulders. "After the rescue, I wasn't relieved or grateful—I felt numb. Then, two hours later, reaction hit me like a sledgehammer, and I fell apart."

Cecily couldn't imagine him falling apart. Not Ryan. A sense of sureness seemed to emanate from him, while his matter-of-fact voice was infinitely comforting. She felt the web of terror begin to disintegrate within her, the nightmare lose its grip. Nothing could hurt her while he held her like this. She moved against him, and the towel around her shifted, reminding her of how skimpily she was dressed.

As the reality of this penetrated, his arms loosened around her. "How do you feel now?" he was asking. When she assured him she felt better, he suggested, "What you need is a good shot of brandy and a good sleep. I don't know if there's any firewater in this motel, but I'll try to find some." He was leaning away from her and smiling, but his bracing tone wasn't matched by the look in his eyes. That look seemed to reach into her heart, and her response to it was of such intensity that it scared her. She got to her feet so hurriedly that she staggered and almost fell.

As quickly as a big cat, he, too, was on his feet and catching her arms to steady her. "Easy." The word was casual, yet the tone in which it was uttered wasn't. He was as afraid for her now as he had been on the mountain, and for a moment his eyes were alive with naked emotion. Finally he loosened his grip and stepped away. "I'll get that brandy."

"Don't go—stay with me." The words came out in a whisper, formed without conscious will. He stopped where he was, and Cecily saw him go tense, hard as rock; she could hear his harsh breathing. *What am I doing,* she asked herself desperately trying to marshal her defenses and finding none. She couldn't tear her eyes away from his.

"When I saw you starting to go over today, it was as if it had been happening to me." He spoke quietly, without emphasis. "I've walked away from death before, and that's affected me, of course. But if something had happened to you, I don't think I could have stood it."

Each word was naked truth. She knew that as surely as she read her own heartbeat. He didn't even touch her—he didn't have to. She could feel his nearness and his need of her like a vital electricity flowing between them. Her brain seethed with conflicting thoughts, but she ignored them. He said, as if the words were torn from him, "My God, if I'd lost you..."

Then they were holding each other. The only reality was his arms encompassing her once more, the melding of softness against male strength. He held her tightly, as if wanting to convince himself she was there, and she lifted her mouth for his kiss.

The kiss was fierce. Liquid heat permeated her bones, turning them to honey. She felt drunk with the remembered taste of him. Clasping her arms around his neck, she stroked the crisp dark hair that grew down over his nape. Smoothed the great shoulders, touched the leanness of his jaw. *Welcome back, Ryan,* she thought. *Welcome, my love.*

"I've been lonely for you." His deep voice whispered an extension of her thought as he touched her mouth and eyes and throat with small, passionate kisses. "I've thought of holding you like this. Wanted you."

Impatient hands unfastened knotted towel around her breasts. It fell to her hips, then to the floor as he drew her to him. His hands roved over her, relearning each curve and line, and his mouth was greedy as it played over her breasts. She felt the stubble of his cheek, tough yet tender against her flesh, and his tongue and mouth working their maddening pleasure on her nipples. *Thought of you. Wanted you.* His words echoed in her pleasure-drugged mind.

"I tried to stay away from you. I thought I could stay away—always could end affairs before. Not now. Not with you. Never with you."

Her heart was hammering an anvil pulse. Her fingers were nervous with hurry as she helped him with his shirt. The stiff buckle of his belt. His jeans. Suddenly they were both wild with hurry, and yet when the barrier of clothing had been removed, they stayed still together for a long tender moment before he lifted her up in his arms and carried her to the bed.

As Ryan lowered Cecily and himself onto the cool sheets, they both spoke at once. "I want—" she began, and he said, "I want you so much. Do you want to? Are you sure?"

She held him close. "Ryan, I've missed you. No, that's not strong enough. It's as though I've been missing a part of me."

They began to kiss and touch again. His mouth took hers, then traced fire over her breasts and her belly and between her thighs. Fire seemed to lick along her flesh, and instinctively her hips began to thrust against his in the dance of love. Kissing her mouth, drawing on her nipples, stroking and loving her with his hands, he finally came to kneel between her thighs. And she kissed his mouth and ran her palms over his lean hips, the muscled buttocks, his male power.

As Cecily caressed him, she felt him tremble in her arms. "If you do that," he whispered, "I can't wait."

"Don't." Her voice seemed thick with the honeyed fire that coursed along her veins. "Oh, Ryan, don't wait."

He held her tightly for a moment before lifting her hips to him. For an instant they seemed to be touching everywhere, and then she moved against him and drew him deep within her satin warmth. They were moving together at last, slowly at first. Then more hurriedly, until the heat of their pleasure became almost pain.

"Ryan," she whispered, "I wish..."

She couldn't articulate, but her heart knew the words. If they could always be together with nothing else intruding. If only—but now she could no longer think. His body was moving so deep within hers that she didn't know anymore where she began and he ended. Her own body was undulating, ripples of ecstasy beginning to build at the center of her being.

As she gave herself up to pleasure that was almost unbearable, he said it. "I love you. You know that, Cecily. I love you."

She opened her eyes and looked into the silver gray of his. She saw the reflection of herself and answered from her bursting heart. "I love you, too. I always have. Oh, Ryan—"

He kissed her quiet as together they burst into flame.

11

CECILY WOKE to darkness, but instinct told her the night was nearly over and dawn was coming. A sense of buoyancy lingered as Ryan held her close. She stirred. "Stay quiet against me, love," he murmured. "I want to feel you close."

She leaned back into his arms, realizing how meshed with him she still was. He had drawn her hips into the cradle of his thighs, the hard, lean length of his body fitting into her back. One of his arms supported her head. With the other hand he stroked her waterfall of hair. "I couldn't get much closer," she murmured.

His free hand trailed down to caress the back of her neck, her back, rubbing lightly over the ridges of her spine. "About time you woke up," he pretended to grumble. "I've been lying here watching you sleep...denying myself when I wanted to do this. And this..."

His touch altered subtly as he smoothed strong hands over her thighs, then upward to circle her breast. She turned to face him, and he kissed her mouth. "You should have woken me," she whispered.

"You needed to rest." There was a protective note in his voice, and his smile had a sweetness that caught at her heart. She stroked his stubbled cheek until he turned his head to kiss her palm. "I love you."

He spoke with a warm and happy assurance that seemed to fill the darkened room with light. "God knows I tried to stay away from you." His voice held a trace of wonder, a hint of laughter as he stroked her back and let his hand wander over the rounded curve of her hips. "I wanted you, Cecily. From the moment I saw you, I knew we'd be lovers. But loving you was something I never intended doing."

"I didn't, either." His caresses were irresistible, and she caught his hands, held them tightly against her breasts. "We lead such different lives, Ryan."

"Not in the way you mean. I'm not used to...loving." Knowing him as she did, she guessed that with that simple admission he'd opened his heart to her. "I meant it when I said I wasn't used to people caring about me or for me. I was used to relying only on myself. On deeper level, I didn't have to care about or worry about anyone else. It was easier just to take what I wanted out of life. And yet, when I met you and saw your warmth and love for Art and the Zolichicks, I was envious."

"Surely there have been people who've mattered in your life. Your parents..."

In the darkness she could feel him smiling, sensed that the smile was wry. "I loved my parents, grew to understand them and eventually forgave them. It's a long time since I needed them, but they always had use for me. They played me against the middle, had no qualms about using their only son as a weapon against each other. My father was true to his creed. He used me whenever he wanted to score on my mother, while mother did the same to him."

Cecily could feel the tension that came with the memories. She thought of the Alexanders playing their power games in their magnificent houses, and of her own home in Clinton, filled with the memories of her mother, of laughter, of simple love. She ached for Ryan, and she kissed him quickly, as if this could take away the hurt. "But the old man, Thomas—the man who taught you about the outdoors?" she persisted.

Now he simply sounded sad. "I did care a lot about Thomas. He was a kind and gentle old man, and he treated me like one of his grandsons. He wanted to take me to visit his family on the reservation one day, but before he could, he died.... Thomas died when I was eight. Mom didn't know that I cried myself to sleep for quite a while after that.

"Don't let it worry you," Ryan said when she held him more tightly to her. "All that happened a long time ago, like the story of Hope Cooper and Lovers' Rest."

But it still hurts you, she thought, and through her wellspring of love for Ryan, she couldn't help a spurt of anger. "It's not fair," she cried. "I know you're strong. I know you can stand on your own—probably you learned to early on. But it's unfair not to have anyone to turn to."

"I have you." And if words were inadequate for what he felt, he began to kiss her mouth and her eyes and neck and shoulders, then bent to rub his cheek between the slopes of her breasts before turning his head to sip the honey of her kissed-tender nipples. His words formed kisses on her skin. "Do you know how sweet you are? Like honey. Like the wind in springtime. I could touch you and taste you and never want to stop."

Like sunlight his voice caressed her, and the ache of sorrow she had felt transferred into desire. "Why stop?" she asked him softly. "We haven't really begun yet."

Wanting to give him pleasure, she pleased herself by first kissing his mouth and flat male nipples, by running her palms lightly over the dark-furred expanse of his chest, by stroking the whipcord leanness of his belly and thighs. Then her fingers curled around the cool hardness of him, caressed and loved him possessively. . .until her name was a deep, growling purr in his throat and his strong body covered hers.

"I love you," he was whispering as she shifted to accommodate him.

It was as if they had loved forever, Cecily thought. What they had begun in words they continued to say with their bodies. The stroke of his sex was an extension of his love for her, and she took him deep within her, letting him fill her. *I love you and will always love you*— The thoughts raged so that he seemed to hear them, and he kissed her until she had no breath or power to think. The warmth of him, the weight and power of him, the beat of his blood and the thrust of his love—these were the perimeters of her universe, and she wanted no other boundary. As she whispered her thoughts, they crested the wave together and floated, still joined, out to sea.

LATER THEY DOZED, and woke again to renew their love before bathing leisurely and drifting as lazily out into a beautiful October morning. Cecily had never seen such a perfect day. The air was crystal cool; the sun made prisms of golden light dance round them. She knew exactly what Ryan meant when he kissed her and said, "It's good to be with you today."

They had intended to make good time, so they set a brisk pace toward the Hudson River and New York, but they couldn't keep to it. The day warmed gradually to Indian-summer temperatures, and they found themselves stopping frequently to admire the color of the autumn leaves. Everything they saw, everything they experienced was magical. Even a less than successful lunch of hamburgers, charred clear through and served on slab-hard buns, made them giggle like children. Ryan shook his head in wonder.

"I've got to be losing it. There's nothing funny about this godawful food."

"Are you sorry you're happy?" Cecily leaned her bright head against him for a moment and felt the surprise in him. Happiness was new to him.

But all he said was, "If this is being in love, God help me. I'm not only going soft in the head, I'm pleased about it."

She had known Ryan to be a hardworking, humorous, adventuresome companion. But she had never felt so completely in tune with him as they rode together in silence, or stopped beside a picturesque part of the road to hold hands and talk. The electricity that had always flowed between them had become an empathy so strong that at times there seemed no need for words. Though Cecily couldn't get enough of Ryan's nearness, she realized she didn't have to touch him. She had never felt so alive and so happy. While riding along she looked yearningly at the dark, commanding figure astride the cycle ahead of her. She wanted the beautiful day to go on forever. At the same time she wanted night to fall so that she could be in his arms again.

That night they stopped at an inn near the New York-Connecticut border and sat in a secluded corner of the quaint, low-ceilinged dining room. Their conversation, like their silences, was wonderfully easy and free. They couldn't seem to talk enough about themselves.

Ryan laughed with Cecily over an anecdote about Art and George, then told her an equally funny story about himself as a boy running away from his father's villa in Greece to try to join a gypsy camp. Later, he entranced her by relating how he had gained one of Toledo's greatest aristocrats as a host for Ryan A. Tours' upcoming December jaunt to Spain. To prepare for that tour, he had walked across the Cantabrian Mountains in northern Spain. Cecily knew he wanted to share the adventure and the pleasure by telling her, but she found she didn't want to look as far ahead as December. And later, after they had made love in the quaint but comfortable four-poster in their room, she knew why: she didn't want to look past the end of this time with Ryan.

Ryan was asleep already, and she looked down at him, feeling the familiar ache of love. The hard lines and planes of his face had softened. Her body was still warm from his touch and his kisses, and she had mapped his lean, powerful form with her hands and mouth, intuiting the pleasure she could evoke by touching here, kissing there. She loved him, and she was happy. Yet she felt restless.

Careful not to disturb him, she got out of bed and walked to the window. Beyond the inn, the world slept. The real world, she amended, where Art waited, where Ryan A. Tours and Raya department stores and all Ryan's other interests waited. She didn't want to think of that world, either. Still restless, she turned from the window, intending to go back to bed. Instead she hesitated, then picked up her bag, pulling out her journal.

As usual, writing gentled her thoughts. Once she had begun, there was so much to say. Of her love for this man, of what he had said to her, of the completion she felt when she was with him. They were different, true, but the differences didn't seem to matter anymore. At least they wouldn't matter on the trail.

And later? Cecily paused, her ballpoint resting on the page, unwilling to think past the here and now, unable not to. Later, she knew, things would change.

"What secrets are you writing down in your diary at this hour?"

She realized Ryan had probably been watching her for some time. He had thrown the cover aside, and against the white bedding his body looked strong and male. Passion tugged at her. Her eyes slid down his body to his returned desire for her.

"You were sleeping," she told him. "I felt wide-awake, and I didn't want to bother you, so I was writing down some of my impressions."

"Come over here.... I'll give you something better than impressions."

At the tender teasing in Ryan's voice, she felt the unease, the questions that had filled her mind slide away. Useless to think of tomorrow when tonight was so sweet. She snapped shut the notebook and returned it and the pen to her luggage.

"Braggart," she said happily as she hurried back into his arms.

THEY SPENT THE NEXT TWO DAYS crossing Connecticut, and because the weather was warmer than it had been even in September, they decided to camp out on their last night in the Connecticut hills. They tried a campground that Ryan had earmarked as a possibility for his tour, a beautiful place almost deserted at this time of year. They had plenty of daylight left to explore the hiking trails that wound alongside a clear, brisk stream and out into an almost-circular glade of sun-warmed trees. They were admiring the glade when Cecily heard a raucous noise.

"Look! The geese are flying."

High above them, gathering in the vee formation of migration, the great birds were honking loudly as they started their journey. "I wonder how it feels to fly like that." His exclamation was full of envy, his heaved sigh ruffling her hair as she leaned against his broad chest. "The old admiral in front must feel the wind resistance like ice water. What fantastic power he must have."

Power—the word nibbled at the edge of her mind, disturbing her contentment. She glanced up at Ryan, almost expecting to see the speculative gleam she had so often glimpsed in his eyes in their early days together. Instead Ryan was thoughtful. "In a day we'll be back in Boston," he said.

"Are you sorry?" she asked, and noted the slight hesitation before he nodded.

"Sorry to see this trip end for us, yes. It seems as if there hasn't been enough time." He turned her toward him, his hands light but sure on her shoulders. "I'll miss the mountains and the valleys, but they'll always be there for us when we come back to them."

It was the first time either of them had mentioned the future or given any indication that their journey of love would continue into the real world. Cecily closed her eyes, listening to the wind, the geese overhead and the beating of his heart. She was suddenly happy, as happy as the bird that, somewhere nearby, sang its liquid notes and then hushed.

"I'll always think of all our days as being like this one, Ryan. It seems so perfect. We're far away from everything and everyone."

"Our day and our world."

He caught her hand and was suddenly urging her down beside him onto the mossy ground at the foot of the trees. The moss and leaves formed a crisp yet soft cushion. She was the one who curved her arms around his neck and kissed him, tenderly at first, then with a growing passion that matched his. His tongue arced against the softness of her inner mouth, tasting, sipping, exploring. She met his kiss with hers, then drew a little away to look up at him doubtfully.

"Here, Ryan?"

"Here, in our world. I want to remember loving you here." His voice was as urgent as the hands that thrust aside her jacket and worked the buttonholes from buttons.

There were so many sensations that accompanied this loving—she was aware of them all. She felt his beloved flesh against her own, the scent and the cool spongy moss and leaves that pressed into her back through her shirt. The mixture of tough and smooth, soft and sharp, was erotic past bearing, as was the rasp of his cheek against her breasts and velvety abdomen. When he teased the buds of her breasts erect, she began to murmur with pleasure.

"You're purring," he breathed against her much-kissed flesh.

He was purring, too, that well-remembered, deep growl of satisfaction when she matched his passion, kissed and caressed his mouth and his bare chest. Soon she was tugging at his belt, then his jeans and briefs, running her hands over the firm muscles of his buttocks and thighs. He wanted to move to undress, but she couldn't bear to have him away from her. She wanted him now.

Never before in all their loving had Cecily felt like this, filled with a heat that sprang inexhaustibly from some hidden spring of molten need. Holding him tight, she kissed his hard belly and thighs and let her lips wander intimately across him. Touching, flicking with her tongue. Loving.

"Cecily, my God, enough—" He caught her and drew her under him, their joining a fierce, dark fever that wouldn't let them be still. They couldn't seem to move quickly enough. She had never felt as full of his desire for her. Their bodies melded so that it seemed they were reaching out to each other, expressing something beyond even the intense physical ecstasy they shared. Something deep and primal was entwining their hearts. Still Cecily yearned for deeper and deeper oneness with him.

She kissed his hands, his mouth, his broad shoulders, scratched his muscled back. "I want you," she told him. "I want this to last. Ryan..."

His kisses rained down on her face. "It'll last," he vowed.

Poised together on the brink of shattering, he grew still within her. They kissed and smiled tremulously at each other. "I love you," she told him, and slowly he began to move again, filling her body, her heart and her universe. For an instant they were completely together in a union that took them over the lip of forever. And as they reached climax together, again and again, Cecily clung to Ryan's promise.

It would last, Cecily told herself. She wasn't at all sure anymore that she could stand a world or a life without Ryan.

12

FINE WEATHER CONTINUED to follow Ryan and Cecily the last leg of their trip through Connecticut, making days as near perfect as they could have hoped for. They spun the trip out as much as possible, spending a night in Hartford and then visiting a pleasant country inn near the Congunond Lakes. They were behind schedule as they finally crossed the state line at Southwick.

Almost as soon as they had crossed into Massachusetts, it began to drizzle. The sky which had been so blue and gold with warmth-giving sun, grew cold and overcast. Cecily tried not to let the damp and the chill affect her spirits, but as they rode Route 2A, which would take them into Boston, she wished her tour with Ryan could have ended in sunshine.

She knew he also was worried about the weather. He had been in communication with the staff of Ryan A. Tours all during the trip. Most recently he had phoned from Hartford to make sure a cocktail reception celebrating their return to the Copley Plaza would go off without a hitch. He didn't want the rain to detract from their arrival. "Still," he said, "you always look lovely, dripping wet or not. We'll give the VIPs and the media their money's worth."

She chuckled at his allusion to their bath at the Bramton, and then her laughter hushed. She had become so used to being with Ryan. After today, that would change.

"I'm going to miss not being with you tonight," Ryan said, echoing her disappointment. "But I know your father and the Zolichicks will want to monopolize you for a while." He paused. "The reception is going to be a crazy scene, but I promise to call you later tonight."

She understood the reality of that when they arrived at the Copley Square Plaza. There they were besieged by VIPs, sports personalities, politicians and the media awaiting Ryan's return. He was immediately surrounded, while she was dragged aside by Art and the Zolichicks, who greeted her as if she'd been gone for years. Even when the reception ended and she was leaving with her family, she had no chance to talk with Ryan. His eyes meeting hers across the crush of people told her mutely that he loved her.

Much later he phoned her. The Zolichicks were just about to leave, but when they learned it was Ryan calling, Art insisted on greeting him. Though Edna was too busy to come to the phone, she issued an invitation through George. "It's nothing like you'd get at one of those fancy hotels Ceci's been telling us about, but it'll stick to your ribs!" George boomed.

Cecily practically had to tear the receiver out of George's hands and retreat with it to a quieter corner of the hall. "Sounds like there's one hell of a party going on there," Ryan said somewhat wistfully.

She closed her eyes and wished he was near enough to touch. "Just the family. How are you?"

"Up to my ears in long-distance calls and reports and problems. Boring stuff. I'd rather hear about your evening."

Behind her closed lids she could almost see him. If she breathed deeply she could draw in his distinctive scent. "Edna cooked wonderful linguini, and we all stuffed ourselves," she said. "Then Matt called from the U of Mass and got into an argument with George because he wants to race at Jedborough again, the first weekend in November. George thinks it's much too soon after Matt's crack-up. Then they made me tell them all about our trip, and Art got out his own albums, and we just sat and talked." She lowered her voice. "I miss you...."

"While I was talking business to my people, I kept thinking of holding you in my arms." He sounded both restless and unhappy. "I'd hoped to see you tomorrow, but it turns out I'm going to have to fly to New York tomorrow, then on to Chicago on department-store business. I'll probably be gone a week to ten days. There's nothing I can do about it, but I'll miss you like hell."

"You knew this would happen when you got back to Boston." Cecily had been aware of his business commitments, and she kept her tone free of an inescapable trace of disappointment. "I'm the one who thinks I've landed in the wrong place. I left a sleepy little garage—and I've come back to motorcycle city. Art thinks the world has discovered Leeds."

"The world has good taste." Ryan laughed with her, and then his voice deepened to loving regret. "Keep well, love. I'll call you from New York."

He did call the next day, but she was in Boston running down a part for an Italian import, and when she tried to return his call he wasn't in his hotel. He didn't call the next day. Cecily wasn't bothered, since she knew how busy Ryan would be after his long time away. And when another silent day passed, she reminded herself that he was probably too immersed in intricate business maneuvers to think, let alone have time to telephone.

The trouble was that she thought of him almost constantly. As she discussed a client's new Motor Guzzi with Art or did maintenance on a much-traveled Harley Roadster, Ryan was never far from her mind. She didn't realize how enmeshed she was in thoughts of him until the Friday after her return from the trip.

"Ceci, are you asleep with your eyes open?" Art demanded. "I've asked you for the wrench three times."

"I'm sorry," she said, almost tacking on "Ryan." She answered her father, "Just wool-gathering."

"You're entitled," Art said fondly. He beamed at his daughter, full of pride. "Must be some adjustment, coming home to this mess after the tour."

Home. It was all around her, the warm, comfortable garage, crowded now with machines brought for repair or resale by new customers. All her life the sounds and scent of home had been everything she'd needed or wanted. This was the first time home hadn't been enough to fill her life. She wished she could feel more content.

"George is coming around later to do the books," Art was saying apprehensively. "If I were you, I'd head for the hills." Cecily looked at him in surprise.

"I thought business was booming."

"It is. It's not that. George is going to want me to talk Matt out of racing at Jedborough, and you know how I feel. Once you start running scared of something, you just keep running, so if Matt wants to try again, I'm all for it." Art ran a hand through thinning hair. "George isn't going to like that."

She went to him and kissed his cheek. "He'll end up eating out of your hand." Art looked unconvinced, so she added, "Tell you what. I'll go make a pot of coffee and some of that apple trifle he loves. Then when you and he have had about half an hour together, I'll come in with the food and rescue you."

Art brightened, but only temporarily. "After half an hour of George's yelling, I may need something stronger than coffee," he hinted darkly. "Do we have any firewater in the house?"

"Firewater in the house—" Instantly she remembered the night Ryan had come to bring her comfort and love. It was incredible that almost every word spoken had a double meaning known only to her. She missed him so terribly that the ache of longing was almost physical. It was a struggle to keep her voice light, but she managed. "I'd better bring a peace pipe, instead."

As she left him working, Jon Simonson came riding up for his afternoon's work. He hailed Cecily and told her he was having some difficulty with the clutch of his Honda; together they debated the problem. By the time she went into the house she had regained her balance, and as she put the coffeepot on to perk, she was thinking not only of Jon's clutch but of Matt's BMW. If he was really going to race on it, she really wanted to check it over completely. She heard a car drive up to the garage and stop, at which she smiled wryly. George was here early, she thought. Poor Art.

She started to chop apples and mix flower and sugar and butter for the apple trifle, but her mind stayed with Matt's motorcycle. She should check the suspension, install new spark plugs that would resist overheating. She'd leave it to Art to do the most important job—make George believe that Matt could do what he was setting out to do. People had to believe in people they loved. As she believed in Ryan.

Ryan. Suddenly he became the one reality: Ryan with his dark hair flopping into keen gray eyes. He was so vivid to her that she could sense him here in the kitchen, could almost hear his laughter.

Cecily tried to pull herself back to reality as quick youthful steps came up the back stairs. There was a light knock on the door. Jon, of course, probably come to report that Art and George were at it tooth and nail. Quickly she put the apple crisp in the oven and called over her shoulder for Jon to come in. "Coffee will be ready in a minute," she added.

"But I really didn't come for coffee."

As she whirled in response to the deep voice she found herself in Ryan's arms. He had been so real in her mind that for a moment she wasn't sure where reality ended and fantasy began. But she wasn't about to complain. His arms around her were as strong as ever; his mouth tasted as sweet. And when he drew a little away, his eyes held the remembered light in them. "That's more like what I had in mind," he said with a grin.

As if to reassure herself that he was there, she ran her hands over his arms. The toned muscle was the same. So was his smile. Her voice was husky with pleasure as she asked, "When did you get back to Boston?"

"This afternoon. I was supposed to stay on in Chicago through the weekend, but I sped things up." He rubbed his mouth lightly against hers. "You're a sight for sore eyes. Infinitely preferable to figures and reports and earnest types in three-piece suits. I've missed you."

His last words were a deep-throated purr. She felt her body respond to it even before his mouth claimed hers once more. Her back arched against his hands, her breasts pressed soft against his hardness. "Tell me about it," she whispered against his lips.

"I mean to. Not here, though. I came here to kidnap you for the evening. In style, for a change, so I brought wheels other than the Electra Glide."

Before she could reply, there was another knock on the door, and Jon called out, "Hey, Cecily, Art and George are yelling at each other in the shop. Maybe you'd better come out and cool them down."

Cecily's eyes brimmed with laughter, sparkling up at Ryan. "I think I'm going to enjoy being kidnapped." She stepped away from him and looked down at her work overalls ruefully, then at the black 'Vette that was parked beside the shop. "Give me a minute to change."

"Sure you don't need any help? I could use a little...feedback." It was so good to be with him, to share warmth and laughter. She felt alive in a way she hadn't since she'd last seen him at the reception.

"Your kind of 'help' will get us both in trouble." She kissed the hard line of his jaw and then stepped back out of reach. "Go talk to George and Art, instead. Make yourself useful."

"To think I left a perfectly comfortable business meeting for this." He groaned, though his eyes danced. "I've never refereed a fight before, but I'll try."

He did more than that. When Cecily had finished dressing and had carried the refreshments down to the garage, she found Art and George deep in conversation with Ryan. Though George's mustache was still somewhat aquiver, he seemed almost calm as he asked questions about Ryan's coming tour in Spain. The older men beamed at Cecily as she entered, and they both peaceably escorted her and Ryan to his Corvette.

"It's going to feel strange not to be traveling on a motorcycle," she said as Ryan opened the door for her. She waved goodbye to George and her father. "How did you get those two to call a truce so fast?"

He shrugged. "George was obviously worried about his son racing. I told him I thought Matt was a good racer, got Art talking about some of his earlier training, and George finally agreed that Matt should have another go at Jedborough." Having witnessed Ryan's success with talking people into seeing his point of view, Cecily guessed it hadn't been hard to convince George. "Then they asked me about Ryan A. Tours' adventure in Spain this December—and Art told me he's going to England." Ryan paused. "He said he wanted you to go with him."

"He does, but I'm not going, unfortunately. Jon is new and only comes in the afternoons, and we have so much work to do. Also, with Matt racing, the Zolichicks will need moral support."

"I'm glad you're staying home." He reached out and took her hand, holding it firmly in his strong cool clasp. "I don't think I handle being away from you too well. I've missed you more than I thought I could miss anyone. I picked up the telephone several times, but I couldn't bear to hear your voice and not be able to touch you. Does that make sense?"

"I'm not sure it needs to make sense." Cecily only knew that she was radiantly, wonderfully happy now that he was here. She leaned back into the soft leather of the car seat, watching him, loving the strong line of his profile, the concentration with which he drove, the way he carried himself. She was so content just to be with him that it didn't matter where they were going. It wasn't until they were driving into Boston that she questioned him.

"You're being kidnapped, and you should know what that means," he told her. "Beast that I am, I'm taking you to my lair. First, I'll wine and dine you, and then I'm going to take advantage of your youth and innocence." She couldn't help laughing at his leer, but the thought of being in his arms made her pulses leap.

"We could skip the wine and food," she murmured.

He pretended outrage. "And make a liar out of me? I swore up and down to Art and George that I was taking you someplace fancy. I just didn't tell them where."

She had known Ryan maintained residences around the country, including Boston, and she wasn't surprised to find that his condo in Back Bay was both spacious and furnished with the elegance that had marked his executive office. The sunken living room was decorated in shades of white and led up to a dining area, the table set for two with Waterford crystal and gleaming china. An enormous bouquet of roses splashed color from a glass vase that she was almost sure was a Steuben, and more flowers brightened the hallway that she could see leading to what must be the bedroom.

She looked around her with pleasure. "I like your lair."

He came to stand behind her, wrapping his arms around her waist and resting his chin against her hair. "I'm glad, but as they say in the movies, 'You ain't seen nothing yet.' I have ulterior motives for bringing you here."

"As you said before," she murmured, leaning back against him. The feel of his strong body against her back and hips was wonderful, sensual. "What exactly have you in mind?"

"Come this way, and you'll see." To her surprise, he guided her to a large and extremely modern kitchen. "You're going to watch me make the Ryan Alexander steak deluxe."

"Is it better than Ryan Alexander stew?" Though she was teasing him she could tell that he'd gone to a great deal of trouble. A large wooden salad bowl heaped with the finest vegetables stood on the butcher-block table in the center of the kitchen, while near it a basket held what looked to be fresh sourdough bread. Lovely, eggshell-thin Meissen bowls held fresh strawberries; an empty silver wine bucket stood close by. "Ryan, everything looks lovely."

"The way to a woman's heart is through her stomach." When she asked if she could help, he wouldn't let her. He pulled up a chair for her, and from it she watched as he competently grilled succulent-looking steaks.

If the meal wasn't perfection, it was close. The salad was icy and crisp, the omelet and steak delicious, and the bread was so good that she accused him of having had it flown in from San Francisco. He only smiled and poured champagne into her glass, saying, "I intend to make up for neglecting you."

"You didn't neglect me." Now that they were together, she could hardly believe they had ever been apart, that she had ever been lonely. His nearness, the touch of his hand, the promise of love to come—those were her only realities. "You're a busy man. I know that. I wouldn't want to live in your pocket, Ryan. That would never work for either of us. Besides, we've been pretty busy at Leeds, too. Thanks largely to the publicity from the trip."

He was quiet for a moment, and knowing him as Cecily did, she realized he was searching for words. "We've both been busy," he said slowly. "And it's going to get busier. I have to go to Spain in a few days, Cecily."

"You mean for Ryan A. Tours." She tried to keep her voice even, when she felt as if she'd stepped into ice water. He nodded, "How long will you be gone?"

"For at least six weeks."

"So long..." She hadn't meant to say it out loud, but she couldn't help it. The sense of well-being and joy that had come with Ryan's presence seemed to dull. She felt the chill of that remembered loneliness. Soon, however, she rallied. Hadn't she just told him she wouldn't live in his pocket? Forcing a smile, she said, "I envy you. It's going to be a wonderful tour."

"It will—but only if you come with me."

Her eyes flew up to his and were caught and held by their intensity. Warmth and tenderness silvered the sea-gray depths as he went on. "Think of making love under the moon in Almansa. And in Andalusia, of watching a flamenco that will sizzle with such passion that the air will char around us." His deep voice was passionate, also, and as tender as a love song. She held her breath as he continued. "We'll walk down the steps of the villa of my friend the Marquis de Aquila-Monteverde in Toledo. We'll enjoy gardens designed during the days of the conquistadores."

She let out her breath in a sigh. "It sounds wonderful. Magical. But I don't think—"

"The trick is not to think. Just go with it, let it happen." He took her hand in his and turned it over, kissing the palm. His warm mouth evoked other kisses, and she shivered as the sensuous memories crowded close.

Weakly she said, "I promised Art that I'd stay with the shop...."

"The shop will manage without you. I can't. Nothing in Spain will have any meaning without you. I don't want to be away from you."

Listening to him, Cecily found her very reasonable, logical objections losing shape and fading away. Ryan was right. Nothing anywhere would have meaning without him. "I don't want to be away from you, either," she whispered.

His smile was full of warm pleasure, yet it was oddly sweet, reminding her of the loving and the openhearted tenderness that had melded them on the trail. He got to his feet and came around to where she sat, drawing her up into the circle of his arms. "They say Spain is a wonderful country for a honeymoon," he told her.

"'Honeymoon'?" she repeated huskily. Shaken, she leaned back and looked up at him.

He kissed her hair and her forehead, worked down to her eyes and the corner of her mouth. "I'm a smart businessman, my darling. I'm not about to let the best thing that ever came into my life get away from me."

"Do I look as if I'm trying to get away?" she murmured.

"You can't. I have you where I want you." He kissed her quickly, softly many times, the caress imbued with a passionate tenderness. "Besides, no woman in her right mind would turn down a man who can cook. You'll marry me, won't you?"

Cecily was light-headed and wonderfully happy. Her smile was dazzling, joyous. "What do you think?"

"I think we've talked enough." Their lips met, touched, united. Held tightly to him, Cecily felt the heat of wanting him clear through to her bones. For a long moment they stood swaying together, before he lifted her into his arms with a swift, deft movement and headed for the hall. "I want to tell you how much I've missed you and how much I love you in every way I can."

Their mouths met again, and she was dizzier still with needing him. It was unlike any desire, any passion she had felt before, and it seemed to move through her veins with the beat of her blood. "I love you so much," she whispered.

His voice was rough with feeling. "You showed me what love was, darling, and I learned my lesson well. Waking, asleep, apart, together—touching and not touching. I'm always with you. 'Love' is a weak word for what I feel for you, but it's the only one I know."

His was a promise sweeter and more binding than marriage vows. "We'll find new words together Ryan," she said, "and ways to show how we feel." They kissed once more and then stepped apart, looking deep into each other's eyes. Cecily marveled at what they were sharing, at this moment of perfect understanding.

Then, helping each other with their clothes, they walked hand in hand to Ryan's big bed. When he took her in his arms again and lowered her gently to the cool, smooth sheets, he whispered her name. Then they loved each other, tenderly, passionately. Neither at Lovers' Rest nor later on the trail had they made love like this. Tonight there was no room for doubt, no hint of the poignancy of parting. Absorbed in each other, they touched and kissed and whispered words of love they were sure only they had ever spoken. And when they were joined at last, Cecily knew that tonight not only her body and her heart were one with Ryan's, but also that their essences touched. "Ryan," she sighed. "Ryan..."

His response was a kiss. In his eyes she could see a reflection of her own fulfillment as they exploded together again and again...and drifted into a wilderness of stars.

13

RYAN KILLED his car engine and pulled the vehicle under the shadowy trees that grew beside the garage. He put his arms around Cecily. "I wonder if kissing you here in Clinton will feel different from kissing you in Back Bay?"

"I don't know. We'd better try." Tendrils of fire curled lazily through her as his lips touched her much-kissed mouth. "Feels pretty good," she commented breathlessly.

"*You* feel good." His whisper against her lips was another caress. Suggestively, sensuously, his tongue circled her lips, and his hands caressed her cheek and throat, lowering gradually to curve over the slopes of her breast.

She sighed in both regret and in protest. "Art's waiting for us. We called him from Back Bay and told him we had news, remember?"

"I know." Ryan kissed her again, then drew back. The smile they shared was loving. "I'm having a hard time keeping my hands off you," he confessed.

"Likewise," she assured him, softly.

"There'll be time, my love." His eyes became tender, his kiss gentle. "So. Now we go tell Art."

"If I know him, he's probably guessed. His instincts are pretty good." As they got out of the car and walked arm in arm past the garage and up the front steps, she added, "He'll be glad. He's always liked you."

As she spoke, the door of the house flew open. Art stuck his head outdoors. He gray hair was rumpled, and his mild eyes were snapping with excitement. "Here you are—finally."

Cecily hugged her father, and then saw over his shoulder that he'd been busy. The living room had been vacuumed and newspapers and magazines whisked out of sight. Beyond, in the dining alcove, cups and plates and silverwear had been set. "You needn't have gone to all this trouble," she exclaimed.

Art beamed. "From the way you sounded over the phone, it was a happy occasion." Wrapping one arm around Cecily, he hooked the other through Ryan's and drew them both into the house. "Besides, we may have company."

"You've invited the Zolichicks?" Mischief brimmed in Cecily's eyes as she glanced at Ryan. George would call for champagne and make awful, long speeches, and Edna would start planning the wedding. Well, it was time Ryan got to know what her family was like.

To her surprise, Art shook his head. "No, not the Zolichicks. It's that editor, that Leonard Coxe from *Intro*."

"From *Intro*—" Cecily actually had to think a moment before she made the connection. Since returning to Clinton, she'd forgotten completely about Leonard Coxe and his magazine. Forgotten, too, about calling him to explain that she couldn't write his article.

Art was saying, "He telephoned soon after you called, Ceci. He asked if he could possibly come by and talk to you tonight, and I didn't think you'd mind."

"He's coming here?" Cecily demanded, while at the same time Ryan spoke with some annoyance.

"*Intro* have interviewed me before this—business exposés only—and Coxe is no fool. He should know better than to intrude on my private life or those of my friends."

The secret soul of Ryan Alexander... The echo of those long-ago words entered Cecily's mind like a presentiment of danger. Hastily she explained, "This is my fault. I forgot about Mr. Coxe. I should have telephone him when we got back from the trip."

"Telephoned him about what?" Ryan asked. He looked bewildered.

Before she could get together words of explanation, Art beamed. "Didn't Ceci tell you? This Coxe person wants her to write an article for *Intro*. You know, an article about her trip with you."

"An article for *Intro*." Cecily felt a sinking sensation in the pit of her stomach, and it worsened as she registered the altered note in Ryan's voice. He sounded too cool. He chose his words too carefully. "You never mentioned any of this before, Cecily."

"The article wasn't my idea, and I wasn't sure I'd do it." Why, she wondered, wouldn't her mind work more quickly or clearly? Her thoughts seemed to be moving through mush. "Mr. Coxe suggested I wait and see—"

"She took notes and everything, even kept a journal." Proud to show off his daughter's cleverness, Art didn't notice the hardening of Ryan's expression, but she did.

"The journal you kept—that was for Coxe, too?" His tone was even, but it made her shiver. It reminded her of how he'd sounded on the night she had defied him and the Swindyne consortium. "Then the article was going to be a travelogue?"

Beginning to be concerned, Art spoke up eagerly, only making the situation worse. "Like she said, Cecily didn't go looking for Coxe, Ryan, it was his idea. He said that everything you did or thought was news, that what she learned about what made you tick on the trip would interest *Intro*'s readers."

"And so you decided to research and write a personal article based on what you had learned during our time together." No mistaking it now—Ryan's voice was deadly. "I see."

He didn't see, not at all, but when she tried again to explain, the look in his eyes chilled her into silence. Hard as sea-washed agate, those eyes gazed down at her as if she were a loathsome stranger. Somehow she found her voice. "I decided a long time ago not to write that article, Ryan."

He dismissed her protest. "Of course you weren't going to write it. By marrying me you'd have gotten your hands on a fortune, not just on the paltry thousands *Intro* would have paid you for the intimate details of my life." His laughter was a harsh bark. "It must have delighted and amused you when I trusted you with secrets I've never told anyone else."

He began to walk toward the door. Cecily watched him in horror, finally crying out, "Will you please listen to me? There was never going to be an article. Coxe did approach me, yes, but I said right from the start that I would write it only if you approved it first. That I might not write it at all."

He turned swiftly, and his tone stung like a whiplash. "Damn right you wouldn't. My lawyers are the best in the country, and both you and *Intro* would have been slapped with a lawsuit that would have ruined you both. You're out of your league, Cecily. Best to stick to things you know and do so well."

She heard the door slam and then Art's bewildered voice, demanding to know what was going on. She couldn't stop to tell him now. She couldn't let Ryan leave with this terrible misunderstanding between them. Cecily left Art standing there in the hallway, running through the kitchen door and outside. In the dim porch light she could see Ryan walking toward the parked 'Vette. Calling his name, she hurried down the driveway. For a moment she was afraid he would ignore her, but after a second's hesitation, he stopped and waited.

"Please, Ryan, we need to talk."

"Why bother? I think we both have a good idea of what's going on."

Anger spurted in her as she realized he'd already judged and condemned her. "Why can't you even hear me out? Are you afraid to listen?"

That pulled him up short. He folded his arms across his chest and leaned back against the 'Vette. "Talk away."

His shadow seemed to merge with the dark bulk of the car, and there was more than a hint of menace in his silence. Defiance edged her voice as she said, "I wasn't lying when I told you there wasn't going to be an article. I meant to call Coxe when I got back to Boston, but we've been incredibly busy, and I forgot."

"And your journal?" The question was calmly asked, but Cecily sensed the hard, driving anger behind the words. "'What Ryan and I did in bed' isn't the kind of thing I'd expect *Intro* to print," he went on, "but the tabloids would have handed over small fortunes for that kind of drivel. I can see why you'd take notes. You couldn't afford to forget anything, could you?"

She felt sickened. "You think I would do that?"

"No wonder you were so interested in my parents, in Thomas, in everything that concerned me. And here I thought it was love."

The cynicism of his words filled her with despair, but now she was angry, too, and this steadied her voice. "I've never lied to you—and if you thought it through you'd know it, too. The trouble is that you can't trust me. If you think I could do something like this, you could never have loved me, either." In spite of herself, a quaver had invaded her voice. "You think everybody is like you, playing power games...."

Silence closed in on them as her voice died away. She could hear Ryan's even breathing and the autumn crickets busy in the grass by the treees. And that was all. He wasn't going to answer her. A cold wind wrapped itself around her. She shivered, suddenly chilled. He wasn't about to answer her. He didn't believe her. He only stood there, a wordless, implacable shadow, a stranger in whom she saw not one trace of the man she loved so deeply.

Close to tears, she turned away to walk toward the house. Every part of her, body, spirit and heart felt lacerated. She seemed to be walking in a nightmare.

Any moment now, she thought numbly, she would wake up with his arms around her.

Cecily heard his step behind her, and renewed hope made her turn quickly to him. She wanted nothing more than for him to take her in his arms, but he didn't touch her. His face was in shadow, yet when he spoke there was no mistaking his tone. "You're a clever woman, Cecily," he said. "I don't really blame you, either. All you did was to strike while the iron was hot and sell out to the highest bidder. My father would be proud of you."

His jeering finally drew blood. Too hurt herself to hear the pain that overshadowed his mockery, she glared into Ryan's face. Somehow she made her voice as hard as his. "You can go straight to the devil, Ryan Alexander. And I hope I never see you again."

THAT EVENING she met with Leonard Coxe to tell him there would be no article. Later she destroyed her journal, and as she tore page after page out of the notebook she had kept for so long, she knew the journey through the mountains was over and must be forgotten. Reality was what she had to live with from now on.

She plunged into work, and for the first few weeks things went well. She was busy helping Art get his passport renewed, shopping with him, assuaging his doubts about going to England alone. He was still trying to argue her into accompanying him when they drove to Logan Airport in early November. Even while he was checking his baggage he didn't give up completely.

"You could still follow me to England," he pointed out. "It doesn't seem right going alone. Remember when we used to pull that atlas out and look at all the places we were traveling to, you and me? I wish you were going with me, that's for sure."

Cecily wished it, too, and yet she knew that even if she weren't needed at the shop, such a trip wouldn't live up to her dreams. The part of her that had yearned for adventure, the joyous, youthful part had disappeared forever since Ryan—but she mustn't think of him. He had no part in her life now or ever again.

"You'll be back before you know it, and you'll have all kinds of adventures to share," she told him, hugging her father tightly. "Anyway, I couldn't go. What would the Zolichicks do without me?"

She thought Art would smile at that, but he didn't. He watched her with a worried expression in his eyes. "Are you sure it's Matt's racing that keeps you home?" he finally aksed. "I promised myself I wasn't going to pry, but—Ryan's in Spain, Ceci. He's gone."

"Ryan has nothing to do with my staying here. We worked together, and for a while we thought we cared about each other. That's all there was to it."

"You mean, that's all you're going to tell me." He shook his head at her. "Is that why you change the subject whenever he's mentioned these days? Ceci, I've seen you put down the newspaper when there's an article about him in it, or get up and go away when anything about his tour in Spain comes on the news. You're a grown woman, sure, but I can't help hurting when you hurt." His voice grew sad. "I still don't know exactly what happened between you and Ryan that night, but I can guess it was some misunderstanding. It's not worth losing someone you love over a misunderstanding."

"I'm afraid it's not quite that simple." Nothing could ever be simple with a man like Ryan, who had said he loved her but didn't trust her. Still, for a while they had been so very close it had seemed that nothing could ever come between them. The pain of that thought went deep.

Art continued as if she hadn't spoken. "You still love him, though. I see all the signs, Ceci. You don't laugh as much as you used to, and your eyes are sad." He paused. "Even George notices that you don't want to go over to his place much anymore, or do any of the things you used to enjoy."

She started to protest but he insisted, "There's a time when your home and your family aren't enough to fill your life anymore. There's a time when you want to be with someone else so bad it hurts. I know you loved Ryan, and for what it's worth, I'm sure he loved you, too. As I said, I don't know exactly what happened to spoil things, but don't you regret loving him. Too many people never love at all."

She hated the tug of pain in her heart as she said, "Meanwhile you'd better catch your flight before it takes off without you."

Finally Art left. She watched him walk away through the covered ramp, swallowing the lump in her throat as he disappeared. An old loneliness came surging back to fill her heart; with it came an ache for something she didn't dare name.

"Excuse me."

The deep voice behind her shocked her, momentarily robbed her of breath. It couldn't be, she thought. He was in Spain. For a moment possibilities flooded her mind; her blood raced and her pulses sang. Then she whirled and saw an anxious, bearded young man with knapsack slung over his shouder.

"Sorry," he was saying, "but which way is Gate 32? My flight's been announced, and I can't seem to find it."

Her heart was hammering as she directed him, but her voice was calm and capable. When he had gone she started walking quickly down the airport corridor. She was furious at herself for the spurt of blind joy that had raced through her veins when she had thought she'd recognized Ryan's voice. Now the loneliness was worse, had become a wrenching ache that told her how desperately she missed him.

She had meant it when she said he had gone from her life. There was no percentage in fooling herself. She thought with dispassion of him enjoying the sights and adventures and the women of Spain, then forced her mind beyond him to the busy days ahead. There was so much to do at the shop, so much yet to do to prepare Matt Zolichick for the race in Jedborough that weekend.

Yet Cecily still found herself looking further ahead, confronting all the days and years that would make up the rest of her life. Time stretched forever like a corridor, and though she knew she would fill it with work and family, Art was right. Work wasn't enough—and neither were those she loved at home. Nor was the riding school she and Art might start. She might be happy in her work. She might find contentment, pleasure, even a sense of accomplishment. But something in her deepest and most honest self told her there could be no dizzy heights of joy, no explosive, shattering esctasy or tender delight, no coming together in completion with another part of herself. Never again. Not without Ryan.

For a long moment she held the thought, then slowly let it go. She would have to learn to live without him, and she'd do it, too. In the pine barrens, Mary Gregory has spoken of the loss of her child. In Cecily's own case, she had to rework her life around the empty space left by Ryan. And, she thought defiantly, she would start by helping Matt Zolichick win his race in Jedborough.

That was easier said than done. In Art's absence, she spent the next few days juggling the work at the shop and reassuring George and Edna. When Matt got back from school early on Friday, she left the running of the shop to Jon Simonson and rode with Matt to a track near Clinton. There, Matt tested his BMW, and the motorcycle ran so well that Cecily was sure it was up to the race.

She wasn't so sure about the rider. Matt seemed full of confidence, but she could hear doubt in his voice. His riding style was rough, too, unlike his usual technique. She hoped his nerves would smooth out as he took his practice runs at Jedborough before the race, but she was also concerned about his downshifting. He didn't seem to be used to his new gearbox.

However, Cecily kept her fears to herself, until day of the race. It was cloudy November day with a cutting wind, and George and Edna and Matt's Peggy, who had all insisted on coming to Jedborough for the event, were bundled up in mufflers and hats. They were all huddling in the pit, waiting for the racers to finish their practice runs, when Matt turned to Cecily. "I wish Art were around to watch me," he said.

His tone held a trace of panic, and she looked up at him, concerned. "Are you feeling okay? Maybe this is too soon for you to race. It's not a big deal, Matt. If you don't feel good about it, skip Jedborough."

Matt was already shaking his head. "Art told me the best thing to do was to get back out on the race-track. Besides, dad has finally calmed down and agreed to my racing." He glanced at his mother and his girlfriend. "I can't back out now."

Listening to Matt, she could hear that hard edge of determination, read in his eyes an expression that jolted her, because it was that same shadowed look she had seen so often in Ryan's eyes. Impatiently she tried to thrust the thought away, but it haunted her.

"It's crazy, I know," Matt added. "I risk my neck by going out and racing when I'm afraid. But if I don't race, I stand to lose a lot more." He tried to grin. "Sounds kinda crazy, huh? But that's the way it is."

There was no use arguing with him, and sighing, Cecily gave him instructions. "Remember to stay on the cam during these practice runs. Your engine is really going like a honey, and that gearbox will work wonders if you just relax and handle it right. Remember that a bad shift in the race will leave you standing still."

The starter was waving at Matt, signaling him onto the track for his warm-up runs. George and Edna stopped shivering long enough to wave at their son. Peggy smiled and blew him a kiss. "Go get 'em, tiger!" she called.

Cecily breathed more easily as Matt started forward, his clutch in and his engine revving. George came to stand beside her, and she said, "He's smoothing out and downshifting really well now." George was silent. "It means a lot for him to have you here."

George pulled at his mustache with both hands, yet once Matt returned to the pit, he gripped his son's shoulder for a moment. There was so much love in that small gesture of acceptance that Cecily felt her throat tighten with a loneliness that was as overwhelming as it was unexpected. Her eyes filled with unwanted tears, and as the loudspeakers announced the next race, she stepped out of the pit and into the cool gray November morning. She could see the race better from here; besides, a racer was sensitive to the vibes around him. She didn't want her despression rubbing off on Matt. Let him be surrounded by his family's love, and by Peggy's, and he'd be a winner for sure.

To her relief, Matt took his first esses beautifully and his lines cleanly. There were several riders ahead of him, but Matt was closing the gap. Soon he was locked in an eye-blurring duel with a Honda rider. Matt would spring ahead; then the Honda would catch up and push frontward.

"Think the BMW will pull ahead?" a voice asked beside her.

Engrossed in the race, Cecily nodded. "He will. I hope so, anyway. He's fast, but he hasn't compromised control." She caught her breath as Matt edged past the Honda. "That's it. Come on, Zolichick. Come on. . . ."

Suddenly she stopped talking, for as she drew breath to shout Matt's name again, she registered the combination of after-shave and leather and clean, vital maleness that could only have one source. For a moment her heart pounded so loudly that it seemed as if the sea itself was roaring through her veins. No. It wasn't possible. Someone who used Ryan's after-shave was standing beside her, that was all. This time she wasn't going to fall apart because of mere coincidence.

Very carefully, very slowly, she turned her head and looked up at the tall man beside her. He smiled. Gray eyes caught the bleak November light and glinted as silver as the sea.

"We can't keep meeting like this," Ryan said.

14

HE WAS THERE in the flesh. Realizing she was staring at him, Cecily blinked rapidly. Her senses were besieged. "What are you doing here?" she demanded.

Instead of answering, he nodded toward the track. "Matt's certainly getting under the paint."

"He's racing well." She hoped she was doing all right herself; at least she had her voice under control. It sounded a lot steadier than she felt, because by being there, he had changed everything. Her bones felt like mush, and her pulse was still thumping agitatedly. Why in God's name wasn't he in Spain?

"I thought you were in Madrid."

"I was until yesterday; I flew in this morning." He showed no sign of jet lag. He looked fit and relaxed, his dark, lean good looks enhanced by the familiar black leathers and boots he'd worn during their motorcycle trip. Thinking of that trip was dangerous, and she quickly concentrated on the trappings of his wealth: his gold Rolex, the heavy signet ring on his hand, small reminders that Ryan Alexander lived in a totally different world and played by very different rules.

She stared hard at the track and saw nothing. "So you've made all your last-minute arrangements for the Spanish tour."

To her surprise, he shook his head. "Not yet. I'm back in Boston on business that couldn't wait, and I thought I should give the Electra Glide a workout."

She frowned at his tone. "Is something wrong with it?"

"I'm not pleased with the way the engine sounds, not pleased with the care it's been getting while I've been away, either. I should have left it with Leeds' Motorcycles, instead of parking it." His bland tone gave no hint that he even remembered all that had happened the last time they'd been together. "I stopped by the shop, and your assistant told me you were at Jedborough with the Zolichicks."

Naturally there was a simple explanation for his presence. Cecily said stiffly, "I'll be glad to look at the Electra Glide, if you wish. Just bring it or have it brought to the shop anytime this week. I'll get to it as soon as I can."

"Good," he said casually, and she thought it wasn't right. It wasn't fair that simply by being near her, he had made her body come awake and alive. She jammed her fisted hands into her overall pockets as he added with friendly interest, "Matt took the line on that curve really well. He's going to come in second or third, I think."

As he spoke, Matt took his final turn and roared across the finish line barely behind the Honda, which was in second place. The Zolichicks and Peggy hurried toward him, and Cecily, too, had started toward the pit area, when Ryan said, "Let them handle things. I need to talk to you."

She was pleased by her outward appearance of calm. "What about?"

He hesitated a moment. "I had a talk with Leonard Coxe a few days ago. He was in Spain covering the opening of a trade fair there, and he explained about that damned article he asked you to consider writing."

"I see," was all she said.

"What I said to you that night was inexcusable."

There was a shout of laughter from the closely grouped Zolichicks, and Cecily watched as Edna and George looked around, obviously searching for her. Their merriment underscored her own misery. Ryan's apology had made things worse, not better. Until he had spoken to Leonard Coxe, Ryan had really believed she could have betrayed their love. He had actually thought of her like that. She was numb, her heart like a dead weight. "It really doesn't matter now," she told him wearily.

He didn't answer and she was glad. Perhaps now that he'd salved his conscience, he'd go away and leave her be. Again she started to walk toward the pit area and her friends. This time he didn't try to stop her. He swung into step with her. "You're looking tired, and you've lost weight. You've been working too hard, Cecily."

The real concern in his voice made her bite her lip. It hurt to bring back memories of what had once been. "Leeds Motorcycles has been doing very well, I'm glad to say. But, no, I haven't been working too hard. Mostly I've been coaching Matt for the races today." She broke off to add, "Listen, that's the second event they're announcing. I hope Matt will do even better in this one."

"Cecily, do you know how much I've missed you?"

The deep voice sliced through her defenses and her small talk leaving her exposed and hurting. Then some instinct of self-preservation called up the memory of their last meeting and she said, "Ryan, what game are you playing with me? You've apologized, and I've said it's all right. That's all we have to say to each other."

"I didn't come just to apologize. I came to—" A roar from the crowd around the track drowned out his words, and he winced. "God, can't we go and talk someplace where we don't have to yell at each other?"

"No." No way was she going anywhere alone with him. If he touched her, if he took her in his arms... "If you want to tell me something, tell me here."

He swore under his breath and then rubbed a hand through his hair. The uncertainty of that gesture surprised her, and at the same time unbalanced her. "I can't seem to stay away from you," he said. "I knew I shouldn't have come to see you, yet I had to." His voice was wrong, too. He didn't sound like a polished, self-assured man of the world—he sounded almost frightened. "I'm still in love with you."

Despised tears came into her eyes. She turned her head away to hide them and stared at the gray November landscape. A line from *Macbeth* filtered through her mind, forgotten until that moment, "My way of life is fall'n into the sere...." Cecily knew that was exactly how it would always be without Ryan. As if withered. But better the loneliness, better gray, dreary days, better the emptiness, than heartbreak. She could bear a lack of joy but not the active pain of loving a man like Ryan.

It was hard to talk through her raw throat, so she didn't. She started to walk away from him. She wasn't surprised to feel his hands on her shoulders, holding her back—she had expected him to stop her. What she hadn't reckoned on was her response to the warmth of his hands. His clasp wasn't hard; she could jerk free easily. The trouble was that she didn't want to. Her sense of imbalance had grown until she felt giddy with it. "Please," she whispered, "just go away, Ryan."

"I'll be damned if I go anywhere until you listen." Low but intense, his voice tumbled over her. "I'm trying to tell you—will you listen—what I didn't have the guts to tell you almost as soon as I left Clinton that night. I wanted to come back and tell you I'd been an idiot for doubting you, and that I loved you. But I was afraid you'd tell me that I'd made you stop caring for me. I couldn't bear to face that, so I stayed away."

Instead of listening to his words, she listened to his voice. It was urgent, turbulent. She sensed that he was speaking with all his heart. She couldn't resist turning to look up into his face, and there she saw fear and naked want. All that Ryan felt and thought was in his eyes.

He was saying, "You call it a game, but you must know it never was. Not ever with you." As if unable to resist touching her, he brushed her cheek lightly with his hand, and the caress seemed to reach down into her heart. If felt too full for her chest; it felt as if it were battering against her ribs. She tried to marshal her defenses against him, find her wits to challenge what he was saying. "Even at the beginning, Cecily, when I told myself that what I felt for you was simple desire, I loved you."

There was a roar from the crowd watching the second race, but she only heard it distantly, an echo on the fringes of her consciousness. "You taught me to love you when I wasn't used to loving anyone—wasn't used to needing, trusting anybody but myself. I love you so much, so intensely, that when I heard about that article for Coxe, I acted irrationally." Again, his fingers brushed her cheek. "I thought I'd made a fool of myself by giving you my heart and soul, that you'd set me up and were using me as my parents did so often. But when I'd calmed down enough to think rationally, I knew I'd been dead wrong."

Listening to him, Cecily felt it was starting again, the wild, surging want of him, the need and the love. Desperately, she tried to hold those feelings in check. She had schooled herself to live without him. It had been hard, but she'd done it. Her life now was quiet, manageable. She was afraid of putting herself at risk again. "No," she whispered.

His face went blank, wiped clean of every emotion. His hands fell away from her. As he stepped backward, she saw him stumble. It pained her to see him like this, this always poised, self-assured man. Again, tears filled her eyes, and she turned away to start walking blindly toward the Zolichicks.

"Cecily!"

His shout roared over the racket of the racing motorcycles. She stopped dead in her tracks. Many people standing in the pit area turned to stare at them, George among them. His mustache was bristling wildly, and his eyes practically bulged, until

Edna gave him a dig in the ribs and forced him to turn away.

"I'll be damned if I'll let you go before I say it all." Ryan's voice was brittle with feeling. "I've told you how I feel. I love you more than I'll ever love another human being. That will never change. Without you, my life will have no meaning. If you want to have time to think, I'll give you all the time you need. If you want me to go right now, I'll do that, too. Whatever you want, I'll do, my love."

The last words were spoken so softly that she might have imagined them. Maybe he hadn't said them at all; maybe she had simply heard them as an echo in her own heart. They broke the last of her control, and tears filled her eyes once more. She averted her head quickly, but he saw them, and she heard him draw a sharp breath as if in pain.

His hand cupped her chin and raised it gently. Then she felt his thumbs brushing away the tears. "I'm sorry. I shouldn't have said it like that. I was afraid this was how you'd feel." He cleared his throat, cleared it again. "The last thing I want to cause you is more sorrow, Cecily, so I'll go. I promise you I'll never bother you again."

He meant it. Having laid open his heart, he would leave at her bidding. And if she knew Ryan, he'd never look back. He would continue building financial empires. He would remain the envy of every man and every woman's fantasy. But like her, he would be empty. Alone.

Ryan stepped away from her as if to go at once, and Cecily felt her heart cry out. She didn't want him to go. He loved her, and now she knew he trusted her. The trust wasn't just in the matter of that foolish article, either. He had believed in her enough to be completely honest, no matter what the cost or the pain. If he trusted her like this, how could she hold back?

She reached for his hands and caught them, leaned foreward until her forehead rested against his shoulder. She drew in a deep breath of the beloved scent of leather and after-shave and Ryan. "Until you came back I'd convinced myself I could live without you. Now I know I can't."

There was a moment's silence as he registered her words, and then she heard him exhale a pent-up breath. His arms went around her, not to crush her but to enfold her slowly, adoringly, carefully, as if gathering to him a precious lost part of himself. Unaware of the crowd, she lifted her face to his, and as his mouth sought hers, she knew nothing mattered but being held against him like this, being kissed like this. Their mouths adored each other, their tongues touched, their breaths mingled. Wishing to be even closer, to become one, they clung until lack of oxygen finally made them draw apart.

"I thought I'd remembered how good you feel and taste and smell," Ryan finally said. "I was wrong. I'm going to need a lot of reminding."

She smiled as she heard the resurgence of his old confidence in his voice. "I've missed you," she murmured against his shoulder.

"No more separations. When we're married, we take all our long trips together." She pulled a little away to look up at him, and he said, "Well, the short business trips can't be helped. I have obligations, you have yours. You said once that we couldn't live in each other's pockets. But for anything over a few days, I want my wife with me. You agree, don't you?"

"'Your wife.'" As she tested the words, the old warnings awakened in her mind. She thought of his wealth and his influence and power; she thought of risks. Though she knew now she couldn't live without him, life with Ryan would still hold risks, because they were so different and came from backgrounds that were so far apart. Then, she thought of the love that had brought them together in spite of all those differences, and the warning voices died away. A love like that was worth more than a few risks.

"'Your wife,'" she murmured again, liking the sound this time, but before she could continue there was such a loud roar from the crowd watching the second race, that she turned around. Matt Zolichick was coming hell-bent for leather down the final stretch of raceway, and in this race he was in the lead. This time he was going to place first! As he roared across the finish line, Cecily saw George beginning a Zolichick victory dance.

Through the noise she heard Ryan's voice close to her ear. "You'll be more than my wife, love. You're my partner, my heart, my quiet hills, my magic valleys, my other self. You're Lovers' Rest to me and always will be. I want to be those things to you, too, today, tomorrow and forever." He was smiling, but she knew instinctively that he'd never been so serious in his life.

She drew a deep breath of pure happiness. "You already are everything to me," she told him. "You always have been." And the roar of victory behind them seemed to swell into a paean as they sealed their new contract with a kiss.

COMING NEXT MONTH

#85 LIFETIME AFFAIR Patt Parrish

Ben and Caroline were neighbors battling a storm together to save his beach house from destruction. And when the waves subsided, it was clear that the attraction between them was as inevitable as the tides. . . .

#86 WITHOUT A HITCH Marion Smith Collins

She was footloose and freewheeling down the interstate to a new life in Florida. But one glance in her rearview mirror and Libby found herself rerouted. Suddenly, falling in love was an unavoidable detour!

#87 FIRST THINGS FIRST Barbara Delinsky

Chelsea's job was to track down missing children—not runaway executives. But the moment she found the renegade, hidden away in a remote Mexican village, she knew what she'd been searching for . . . all her life.

#88 WINNING HEARTS Gloria Douglas

Six years ago Elizabeth's childish advances had been spurned by rugged John Logan. Now a glamorous model, she was ready to take on the arrogant cattleman. The result was an electrifying showdown!

OFFICIAL RULES

1. NO PURCHASE NECESSARY. To enter, complete the official entry/order form. Be sure to indicate whether or not you wish to take advantage of our subscription offer.
2. Entry blanks have been preselected for the prizes offered. Your response will be checked to see if you are a winner. In the event that these preselected responses are not claimed, a random drawing will be held from all entries received to award not less than $150,000 in prizes. This is in addition to any free, surprise or mystery gifts which might be offered. Versions of this sweepstakes with different prizes will appear in Preview Service Mailings by Harlequin Books and their affiliates. Winners selected will receive the prize offered in their sweepstakes brochure.
3. This promotion is being conducted under the supervision of Marden-Kane, an independent judging organization. By entering the sweepstakes, each entrant accepts and agrees to be bound by these rules and the decisions of the judges, which shall be final and binding. Odds of winning in the random drawing are dependent upon the total number of entries received. Taxes, if any, are the sole responsibility of the prize winners. Prizes are nontransferable. All entries must be received by August 31, 1986.
4. The following prizes will be awarded:
   - (1) Grand Prize: Rolls-Royce™ *or* $100,000 Cash! (Rolls-Royce being offered by permission of Rolls-Royce Motors Inc.)
   - (1) Second Prize: A trip for two to Paris for 7 days/6 nights. Trip includes air transportation on the Concorde, hotel accommodations...PLUS...$5,000 spending money!
   - (1) Third Prize: A luxurious Mink Coat!
5. This offer is open to residents of the U.S. and Canada, 18 years or older, except employees of Harlequin Books, its affiliates, subsidiaries, Marden-Kane and all other agencies and persons connected with conducting this sweepstakes. All Federal, State and local laws apply. Void in the province of Quebec and wherever prohibited or restricted by law. Winners will be notified by mail and may be required to execute an affidavit of eligibility and release, which must be returned within 14 days after notification. Canadian winners will be required to answer a skill-testing question. Winners consent to the use of their name, photograph and/or likeness for advertising and publicity purposes in conjunction with this and similar promotions without additional compensation. One prize per family or household.
6. For a list of our most current prize winners, send a stamped, self-addressed envelope to: WINNERS LIST, c/o Marden-Kane, P.O. Box 10404, Long Island City, New York 11101

SWRL•A•1

SPECIAL LIMITED-TIME OFFER

Mail to **Harlequin Reader Service®**

In the U.S.
2504 West Southern Ave.
Tempe, AZ 85282

In Canada
P.O. Box 2800, Station "A"
5170 Yonge Street
Willowdale, Ontario M2N 6J3

YES! Please send me 4 free Harlequin Temptation® novels and my free surprise gift. Then send me 4 brand-new novels every month as they come off the presses. Bill me at the low price of $1.99 each—a 13% saving off the retail price. There are no shipping, handling or other hidden costs. There is no minimum number of books I must purchase. I can always return a shipment and cancel at any time. Even if I never buy another book from Harlequin, the 4 free novels and the surprise gift are mine to keep forever.

Name (PLEASE PRINT)

Address Apt. No.

City State/Prov. Zip/Postal Code

This offer is limited to one order per household and not valid to present subscribers. Price is subject to change. DOHT–SUB–1